The fates must be conspiring against her

A mechanical problem in her Cessna had given Nicole no choice but to spend the night at Matthew's remote campsite.

"Thank you for your offer of a berth on your boat," she managed to say impersonally, as he rummaged in the luggage compartment of the plane for her sleeping bag. "But I'd rather stay here for the night."

"Look here." His voice was cool, horribly reasonable. "Just because we don't exactly like each other much— If you sleep out here you'll be miserable by morning. And I can't fly that plane out."

Nicole bit her lip. She was not sure she could handle a night in such close quarters with him—sleeping on the same boat, hearing him breathe, the sound of him turning in his sleep, her own unexpected sensual awareness of him...

VANESSA GRANT started writing her first romance at the age of twelve and hasn't forgotten the excitement of having a love story come to life on paper. Currently she teaches business at a community college, but she and her husband are refitting the forty-six-foot yacht they live on with their sons for a world cruise some time in the future. Vanessa believes in love. "After all," she confides, "the most exciting love story I know of is my own."

Books by Vanessa Grant

HARLEQUIN PRESENTS

895—STORM
1088—JENNY'S TURN
1112—STRAY LADY
1179—TAKEOVER MAN

HARLEQUIN ROMANCE

2888—THE CHAUVINIST

VANESSA GRANT

stranded heart

Harlequin Books

TORONTO • NEW YORK • LONDON
AMSTERDAM • PARIS • SYDNEY • HAMBURG
STOCKHOLM • ATHENS • TOKYO • MILAN

This book is dedicated
to all the people who lived in and loved
the remote island town of Tasu
in the days before the mine closed

and to Cameron and Grant
with love

Harlequin Presents first edition October 1989
ISBN 0-373-11209-2

Original hardcover edition published in 1988
by Mills & Boon Limited

Printed in U.S.A.

CHAPTER ONE

'THROW me a line! You can raft up here!'

The boy on the foredeck of the sleek fibreglass yacht had his hand outstretched for a line, his red-blond hair brilliantly soft in the sun.

A few feet away, on a wooden sloop, Matt spun his wheel with calloused hands, throwing the engine into reverse and giving just the right combination of rudder and engine to stop *Charmaine*'s progress along the floats. He tossed his head to clear his eyes of shaggy brown hair. The hair had been sleekly tidy six months ago when he had last visited a barber. His chin had been clean-shaven then, too, until his razor had disappeared. Once or twice, when he stopped in a town to shop, he had almost bought a new razor. That would have been silly, because sooner or later his was going to turn up.

He was desperate for sleep after the long overnight sail from the mainland, yet still exhilarated from the memory of the wild water of the Hecate Strait surging under him. Sixty miles of water separated the northern mainland of British Columbia from the Queen Charlotte Islands, and Matt had spent those miles in the cockpit, painting pictures in his mind, darkness and shadows, water stretching everywhere with powerful rightness.

With the dawn he had identified the hills of the south island from the chart, then the long, flat depression that stretched along the north island. He had followed the tediously long recommended route between the invisible hazard of the sand bar and the north island. Finally, he had arrived in the harbour of Queen Charlotte City, nestled between the north and south islands. Now his mind was warring between the urge to start painting the dark magic of the Hecate Strait before it faded, and the drugging need for sleep.

Welling up under the drowsiness was an aching pleasure in all he could see. He was powerfully happy that he had come to these islands. He knew already that this place was different, special.

He must sleep. Soon. He should have cast his anchor off in the shallows near the wharfs, caught a few hours' sleep before he docked. It would have been the most prudent course, avoiding the pitfalls of a complex docking when he was exhausted past the peak of efficiency; but he needed to feel the shore under his feet, to soak up the reality of this small town nestled in an island-studded harbour.

So he entered the breakwater, easing *Charmaine* along the fingers filled with boats, then slowly motoring back to the entrance where there was more water for a turn. It came down to two choices. He could tie outside the big fishing-boat, or the shiny yacht that probably belonged to some rich tourist.

Automatically, he made for the fishing-boat. It was common practice in the north to raft boats together two and three deep along the wharfs. This fisherman would not be surprised to come back and find *Charmaine* tied outside him. The white sail-boat, on the other hand, probably came from one of the big yacht clubs in the south. Tie a line to her and her captain would be dashing out on deck, fussing over teak and strangers walking across his decks.

'He's going out later!' shouted the blond boy, his thin arm waving to the massive fishing-boat. 'He's going through the narrows on the high tide this afternoon!'

Matt threw the wheel over and started walking *Charmaine* sideways through the water. He was too damned tired to be woken in three hours' time to let the fisherman out. The shiny white yacht was his mooring, and he hoped to hell the captain was as easygoing as the young crew member, because he was in no mood for a dockside dispute with some rich sailor clad in white yachting trousers.

Once he had the lines fast, he was going to take a twenty-minute tour around the town, get his land legs and wind down a bit. Then bed. God, but his bunk was going to feel good!

Nicole let the Beaver fly itself off the surface of the water. She prided herself in making all her take-offs smooth. It was a game she played, trying to make sure the passengers could not detect the moment the pontoons left the water and flight began. It felt good, the lightness as flight began, the change of feeling of the controls under her hands.

Then the lifting, surging, gentle flight. Rising, banking, the earth dropping away below, a weight freed from her. Freedom.

She was alone in the small seaplane, but it made no difference. The skilful manoeuvre gave her pleasure. If anyone had been in the passenger seat beside her, they would not have known what was inside her mind, her joyful sense of victory over something as simple as a good take-off.

On the outside she was all smooth, controlled woman. She wore jeans and a denim jacket, because she liked the comfort and also because passengers had a hard enough time with the concept of a woman pilot, without her turning up in an elegantly tailored trouser suit. She had enough of that kind of clothing in her hanging locker, but she almost never wore anything but the jeans.

When she was flying, she kept her long, blonde hair tied back, her face free of make-up, shadowed by the cap she wore. She felt a perverse pleasure in making herself plain, dressing roughly, everything a denial of that other life. She had been pleased on the day she flew a charter passenger all the way from Queen Charlotte to the mainland, and later heard that he'd said to Luke: 'That new pilot of yours sure doesn't talk much. He shy?' That was what she wanted, to be noticed so little that the passengers hardly realised she was not a man.

When the radio crackled, Barry's voice didn't say the feminine name, *Nicole*. She was Nick to the pilots and base radio operator at QC Air.

'CF 191, this is base. Do you read me, Nick?'

His voice was clear and crisp, as if he were only a few hundred feet away. In fact, she was eighty miles from the base, but the Beaver had risen high above the islands and, if she could see far enough, she would be looking right at the base antenna.

'191 here.' As she spoke, she banked slightly to adjust her course for the head winds that had developed over the last couple of hours. 'You're loud and clear, Barry. I've dropped off the passengers at Cape St James, and I'm in the air, just over Houston Stewart Channel.' She made a mental calculation, figured in the head winds. 'I'll be in—oh, give it an hour and a half.'

'We've got a pick-up at Cumshewa.'

Nicole frowned, staring ahead. There were fat white clouds nestling against her horizon to the north. She thought they were probably as far away as the Alaskan Aleutians. She didn't want to do another pick-up. You never knew when a simple pick-up would develop complications, and Shane was home alone. This summer was developing into too many flights, too much time in the air for the mother of a young teenager at a loose end.

Lately, Shane had been—she could not quite put her finger on it, but she was a little nervous. She kept reaching for the closeness she had always had with her son, and finding him moody and secretive. It wasn't like him. She had promised herself she would cut her flying hours back.

She had put off talking to Luke about it. Luke was the owner of QC Air—silent, a little taciturn, but he had been a considerate employer, and over the last few years he'd called her whenever he was short-handed. Without Luke's willingness to take on a woman pilot, she and Shane would have had a hard time getting by. She was nervous of asking him to ease off, just for the two months of this summer holiday. That could backfire on her, leave her short of work and money through the winter months.

'CF 191, are you reading me?'

'All right, Barry. I've got you.' Her eyes fell to the airspeed indicator, then past it to estimate her progress over the mountains she had come to know so well. 'I'll do the Cumshewa pick-up on my way in. What have I got there?'

'Two men and a pile of camping gear.'

It sounded simple, but when she landed in the long Cumshewa inlet, she found that one of the men had tracked a deer into the bush with his rifle.

'It's been a wash-out,' complained his unshaven partner. 'We've been out here ten days and seen seventeen deer, and not a flaming one with antlers on. And doe season doesn't open until next week.'

Nicole always felt a sick sorrow when she saw a hunter packing deer carcasses away from the islands. She knew all the arguments. There were too many deer on the islands. With no predators, they had become very small, too populous. She still hated the thought of grown men taking guns out to kill Bambi's sisters. She hid it, and this particular hunter had no idea that her cool face concealed a desire to throw his guns into the ocean.

'I'll wait twenty minutes,' she told him. 'Then, if your friend's not back, I'm flying out without him.'

Fifteen minutes later the missing hunter came out of the bush with the news that he had bagged a deer. 'Better forget us for today,' he told Nicole cheerfully. 'Send out a plane for us in the morning.'

She shrugged and turned away, concealing her irritation and impatience. The sun was shining from the western sky, blue and brilliant, and the islands were bathed in a green, mossy other-worldliness that would have ensnared the coldest heart. Yet she felt a growing alarm. She wished she had not consented to do this pick-up. She should be home. With Shane.

She stepped from the wharf to the pontoon of the plane, doing a silent walk-around inspection, checking twice for clearance on the propeller before starting the Beaver and roaring out of the bay and down the inlet. For once her take-off was faster than it was smooth, and she felt something like panic growing. Was this insanity? Or a mother's instinctive knowledge that something was wrong with her son?

Like that horrible night, so many years ago, when Shane was little more than a baby and she had thought he was dead. Ambulance. Hospital. A fearful, tearing panic that dissolved into frightful waiting for the verdict from the doctors.

When they had sent her home to sleep, she had started a desperate search for Tyler, unknowingly seeking the destruction of her illusions.

God! Something must be terribly wrong to make her feel like this again. Panic would not help, so she forced her breathing slow, forced her hands and eyes to become careful and cautious.

'Hunters,' she told Barry when she threw open the door to the QC Air office half an hour later. Barry looked up at her through owlish glasses that made him look impossibly young and serious, his desk strewn with papers that a busy charter company generated.

'What took so long?'

'They got a deer and decided they'd rather fly back tomorrow.'

Luke had trained Barry well. He had paper and pencil ready, said, 'How long did it tie you up, Nick?' and he was multiplying charter rates by minutes and coming up with answers the hunters would not like when they came out tomorrow.

She pulled off the soft cap and hung it on a hook in the small lounge where the pilots had coffee when they were between flights. She didn't do much coffee-socialising herself. In between flights, she went home to *Island Wanderer* and Shane.

The clasp that held her hair back went into her pocket, and she shook the long, soft cloud of blondeness free around her shoulders.

'I'm off home,' she told Barry as she wrote her hours in on the sheet. 'I'll be back in the morning for the mainland run.' She pushed back the long hair and it settled over her shoulders, caressing the denim of her jacket. She was already moving to the door. 'I've got to get home, Barry. See ya.'

She always walked the half-mile to the government docks. She did not own a car. It usually didn't matter here, with the town so small, and enough friendly people around that a ride was no problem if she and Shane wanted to go to Port Clements or Masset.

Shane would have liked a car, but the money was more than she could manage. It had been a little easier this year, but she had to be prepared for the cost of Shane's schooling and she was unsure if she could manage that without going to Luke and begging for more hours.

But not yet. First let her have these weeks with Shane, this precious summer that seemed so oddly strained. It must have been the knowledge that she had only a few weeks more that had given her that ominous feeling of doom. He was a young man now, and terribly uncomfortable if she touched him or kissed him. She had not managed to get a goodnight kiss out of him in weeks, although she was doing a good job of not showing how much she missed it.

Clinging mother. God, but she was going to miss him when he went away in September! She wished it were right to hold him back, but he wanted to go and it was a good school. And there was always that terrible pressure from his grandmother. The registration in St Michael's had at least defused Mrs Bentham, the old battle-axe!

For perhaps the thousandth time, Nicole told her mother-in-law what she thought of her. Silently. From five hundred miles away. Out of reach of the damned woman's powerful clutches.

She walked down the ramp and out to where her home, *Island Wanderer*, was moored. Her eyes travelled over the fingers, noting that the scruffy sail-boat from Tahiti was still docked out at the end, that Kevin's big fishing seiner was gone, that an old wooden sloop had moored outside her boat.

She stopped in the spot where Kevin's boat had been, now occupied by three small salmon trollers rafted together. She tipped her head a little and tried to be critical as she looked at *Island Wanderer*, her home and

Shane's for the past six years. Thank goodness it was fibreglass and not wood or steel. The sleek, white factory finish did not show that she had been unable to repaint it above decks, although each year she and Shane had taken it out on the tidal grid and repainted the underwater hull with anti-fouling paint.

It had been surprisingly inexpensive to be the owner of a forty-six-foot sail-boat. Of course, she had not been able to afford the insurance once it became hers, and she had got the boat itself through outright blackmail, but it was hers. A home for her son. Ill-gotten perhaps, but legal.

She stepped forward, a slight smile curving her lips, the wind caressing her fair hair and streaming it out behind her.

The smile died as she stepped aboard. She had seen the hatch closed and wondered why Shane would shut himself in on such a sunny day, but assumed that he was inside listening to his latest rock tape on his Walkman, oblivious to the rest of the world. Now, closer, she could see that everything was closed, the hatch and doors locked. Her earlier panic returned, strengthened.

She unlocked the door, swinging it wide and calling, 'Shane? Hi, I'm home!'

He was not there. The boat felt deserted. Her eyes went to the little vinyl note-pad on the passageway.

'Gone to the store for milk.' Shane had not signed his scrawled message, but he had written the words. The trouble was, it was far too late for the store now. She did not know which store, but it hardly mattered. There were only a few shops, and they were all closed by this time. The northern summer sun was still shining, but it was eight o'clock in the evening, and Shane should have been back a long time ago.

She knew she was panicking. Countless non-emergencies in the past were evidence that these things never turned out to be real disasters. He had met a friend, been invited for supper. No. It was their unwritten law, that they never left the boat without each other's knowledge, unless they first wrote a note on the pad. He would have come back first, changed the note to read, 'Gone to Casey's for supper.'

He was talking to one of the fishermen, visiting on another boat. No. He would not have locked up if he were still down here on the floats. Locking up meant he had gone to town, yet not returned.

She went back into Shane's cabin, along the narrow passage. There was no sound, no light, and definitely no teenage boy sprawled on his bunk, plugged into headphones and submerged in stereo sound.

Forward to her own cabin. No Shane.

He was not in the small cabin off the galley, where she had had a workman put in a shelf as a desk for him to do his schoolwork.

Something was terribly wrong.

She would not panic. Not yet. She would check the floats, ask the people standing around on their boats, then go up and find the wharfinger and ask if he'd seen Shane recently. Then the telephone, and Shane's friends.

There was a whole list of things to check before she would be desperate enough to run across to the pretty white building that housed the RCMP and ask about accidents and disasters.

She pushed the hatch back, hearing it bang against its stop and knowing she had to get control of the panic. She never got worked up, never flew into a temper, but right now, if Shane turned up safe, she might just rage at him in her relief.

She smoothed her face and her mind, called again, 'Shane!' although there was no evidence of anyone around outside.

As her shout died away, echoing on the water, a bearded wild man came out of the wooden sloop tied to *Island Wanderer*. He glared at her through eyes that were completely overwhelmed by a shaggy red beard and a wild brown mop of hair. The blue eyes raked her over with an angry hostility.

She forced a smile. 'Good evening. Sorry if I woke you.' Bad-tempered man. Surly anger radiated from him. 'You haven't by any chance seen a fourteen-year-old boy? Blond hair and——'

'Inside.' He jerked his head.

She followed the direction of the abrupt motion to look through his large wheelhouse windows. She saw only a scene of incredible chaos. Shane, inside there? 'Would you please ask him to come home?'

'No.' The man turned away, stepping down into his cockpit and starting through the open doorway.

She called out, her voice cool and commanding, 'Shane! Time for supper. Come on!'

Nothing. Silence. And this man—with a head of hair like that she would have expected him to walk stooped and slow, except that there was no trace of grey anywhere. And he was tall, straight and very thin, all encased in wiry muscles that made him seem suddenly like a dangerous man instead of the harmless eccentric she had thought. A wild man just come down from the mountains. Mountain Man.

His voice was hard, rough. 'He's not coming out. You'd better come and get him. It's time you found out what he's been up to.' Then he was gone, his lean form moving around in silhouette through the windows, the door swinging open behind him.

If Shane was inside, she could not see him. Was this some kind of trap, to lure her in there and then——

She drew her shoulders back rigidly. He might be tall, but he was a thin man, and she had been taking judo for three years now. She had never used it outside of practice, and she would not need it now. She knew how to freeze a man's ardour with her eyes, with cool laughter.

If her son was inside this old boat, why did he not call an answer? She felt a cold anger, because this man was playing with her, and she had no time for futile lies. She had to find Shane.

She stepped over her lifelines, then over the gunwale of his boat. She jumped lightly down into the cockpit. The door was still open. She went through it into the wheelhouse. Oceangoing boats didn't usually have wheelhouses like this, big windows inviting destructive waves. In any case, from the litter of chaos she knew that he did not take this boat to sea, although there were signs that he had recently fastened down some of the mess. She decided that he had just made the crossing of Hecate Strait from the mainland, that by tomorrow this would be even more of a mess as he relaxed from sea conditions.

'Shane's not here. Why——' Her eyes passed him, following his own gaze, her heart racing as she saw grubby running shoes extended into the passageway in the next cabin.

She knew those shoes, the sole half-torn from the toe. She had bought him new runners last week, but he seldom wore them. 'Shane?'

She pushed past the wild man, gasped as his hand gripped her arm. She jerked away, ran down the two wooden steps into the next cabin, stopping in front of her son.

'Shane?' His head was down. He shifted uncomfortably, his awkwardly growing legs too long for the space under the table where he sat. She felt a horrible premonition of disaster. 'Honey?' She swung around the table and slid in beside him. She touched his arm, felt him shrivel into himself and draw back. 'Shane, what's wrong?'

He would not look at her.

'Better tell her.' Mountain Man's voice was cool and hard. She was rapidly learning to hate this man.

Shane shook his head. She wanted to put her arm around him and shelter him from the blazing ice in the man's eyes, but she was increasingly afraid that her son had done something wrong.

Had he somehow damaged this monster's boat? Not likely. The crate wasn't very well maintained as it was. And surely Shane would not be sitting here afraid to look at her if it were simply an honest accident.

'Tell her!' His voice was booming out with the power and authority of a judge.

Shane whispered, 'At home. I'll tell you at home,' and she stood up, pulling his arm, her voice tight and cold for the maniac with long hair and a powerful voice.

'I'm taking my son home. If you have anything to say, I suggest you get it said now before we go.' Something in his eyes made it hard for her to keep the coolness. She focused on the beard, the ragged denim shirt thrown on over a thin T-shirt that must have been around when they launched the Ark. 'No?' she said, rigidly and quickly, giving him no opportunity. 'Then we'll go.'

She went one step, her arm gripping Shane's like death, pulling him along and realising that he was not really co-operating. Damn! Shane was almost as tall as she was, past the stage of being manhandled by a mother.

She freed his arm, said, 'Shane, we're leaving here,' and hoped he was following.

He was thin for a Mountain Man, but he was tall and he blocked her way without seeming to move. His eyes were focused over her shoulder, and she would not have wanted to be needing mercy from him.

'You tell her, or I will.' The words seemed to hit Shane like wounds. Nicole stared from the bearded face that was all cold eyes and hair to the smooth, pale face of her son.

Then she stopped dead and waited for whatever was in Shane's eyes and in the nervous spasm of his throat. He looked down, away from his accuser, and it was long seconds before he looked back to his mother, only to jerk his eyes away.

'I——' His voice was a whisper, breaking. 'I stole—something.'

'You——'

Stealing? Shane stealing?

She knew there had to be a way to handle this, but she had no idea what. He looked battered and hurt. She wanted terribly to take him in her arms and tell him it was all right, yet she knew she must not.

Stealing. Was it the first time? Surely he hadn't been—what had he stolen? From whom?

Shane gave a massive shudder, as if the silence were more painful than the words bursting in her mind. Then he moved, dashing past her and somehow getting past the barrier of the thin Mountain Man.

She supposed she should thank Mountain Man, but she felt no gratitude. She felt sick, worried, and horribly helpless.

For the first time in years she wished desperately that she were not alone, that she had someone to turn to and lean on, someone whose judgement she could trust.

She thought she would explode when Mountain Man touched her again, holding her back while Shane stumbled across the deck and on to his own boat. She jerked back instead, made her eyes as cold as her voice. 'If you would let me past... I have to go to my son. He needs me.'

He stared at her, the blue eyes recording every detail. She tensed when he frowned, the beard quivering with what looked like recognition, but in the end the eyes held only a hint of puzzlement, as if he knew he must have seen her somewhere and could not remember where.

She remembered, although she had no idea which newspaper he had seen her picture in. She had been in all of them, a blazing condemnation of a hard woman. Tyler Bentham's wife.

'Your son needed you earlier.' He sounded like the judge again. 'You should have thought of that when you were out having a good time. Money isn't everything,' he said then, and she understood as he glanced through his porthole at the gleaming white of *Island Wanderer*. He thought her bank account matched the boat. 'The boy needs someone to take some time with him, especially——'

'Mr——' He didn't supply a name, and she did not want to know. 'I—I appreciate your telling me about——' That was a lie, and Nicole did not like lies if they could be avoided. Her eyes sheared away from a magazine lying on the table. Seeing that magazine, she wanted more than ever to get out of here. She changed her words to, 'I had to know, and you can be sure I'll get the rest of the story out of Shane, and that it will never happen again. If there's any damages, anything Shane owes you as——'

She fell silent as he lifted a hand. His hand was like the rest of him, long fingers, calloused and strong. 'He didn't steal anything of mine. I was up in the store and I saw him slipping the—it into his jacket, and——' He shifted, his legs slightly astride, his eyes leaving hers. 'I'd better talk to your husband.'

'You'd better talk to me if you've anything to say.'

He frowned. She thought it was a frown under all the facial hair. Had the man never heard of a razor? 'When is Shane's father going to be home?' he repeated, then his face suddenly became still and intent, as if he could read her thoughts.

She made the muscles of her forehead relax. She had learned something from those days with Tyler. There was only one weapon, only one defence. A cool exterior that no one could penetrate. To do it, you had to believe in it yourself, convince yourself that you did not care what anyone said.

So her voice was toneless and hard. 'He's away right now. If you have something to say to Shane's father, you'd better say it to me.'

She had the satisfaction of seeing him uncomfortable, like a man who wished himself somewhere else. He put a hand to where his cheek would be if it weren't for the beard. He scratched the red shagginess.

'Well?' she demanded. Five seconds. She would give him five seconds, and then she was going to get out of here.

She hoped she could get Shane to talk to her about this. He had been wearing the sulky look that usually meant he would not talk. He kept withdrawing into the silent adolescent that she did not know how to handle. She knew that inside he was shamed and hurt, but somehow she had to know the details, to know what was going on so that she could protect her son and make sure this never happened again.

The Mountain Man took a deep breath, shrugged and said, 'OK, but it would be—— That's what he was stealing. Behind you. On the table.'

She turned to look, more to get her face away from his than to see. She had already seen it, the nakedly voluptuous female breasts blazoned across a shiny cover.

The *Playboy* magazine did not belong to the Mountain Man.

CHAPTER TWO

SHOULD she send him to his grandmother?

She hated the thought of sending Shane away. He would be going so soon in any case. Come September he would be gone from her, only hers in the holidays.

No, not Mrs Bentham. All she would do was spoil Shane and heap all sorts of expensive possessions on him. That would not do anything to strengthen his moral fibre.

She wished she had some way of knowing how serious this was. Did fourteen-year-old boys go through this? Was stealing a stage? She was too damned sheltered to be the mother of an adolescent. Her childhood had contained none of this. Where she'd grown up, there had only been one store, and she could not remember anyone being accused of stealing from it.

Was this the first in a long line of crimes? Was her son actually turning into a criminal? No! She could not believe it, not remembering the hurt in his eyes the night before, and knowing how good-natured and considerate he normally was.

Until lately.

'You're grounded,' she had told him last night. She had been sitting beside his bunk, where she had found him when she left Mountain Man. He had lain there, staring at the wall.

'Shane, you have to understand. This is terribly serious. You're—it's lucky that he caught you.' What was the man's name? She did not want to know, but she could hardly talk about Mountain Man. 'If the man who owns the store—or if the police had been called——'

Shane seemed to shrink. He drew up his knees and turned away from her, staring at the carpet that lined the inner wall of his bunk.

'I don't want you going to the store at all, Shane. I'll do the shopping. If going up there and looking makes you want things that aren't yours——' She felt a wave of heat surging over her face. She remembered Mountain Man's blue eyes dissecting her, and the sexy breasts spread over the magazine cover on his table. Surely Shane—he was just a child. All his friends were boys, and he hadn't even talked about dating a girl. She pushed uncomfortable thoughts away and concentrated on the real issue. The stealing.

That magazine. She would have to get it back, ask Mountain Man for it. She shuddered inwardly, said, 'Shane, tomorrow morning you'll have to go and ask him for the magazine.' She would be happiest if she never saw that man again. 'Then—it's got to go back to the store. It's stolen.' She shuddered at the thought of facing the store owner. He had always said a friendly word to her when she bought milk or eggs. She would hate telling him that——

'It's paid for.' Shane twisted and met her eyes rebelliously. 'He bought it. He—he grabbed me when I was going out the door, and he dragged me over to the magazine rack. Then he—he took it and paid for it, and he held on to me all the time, all the way back here. Then——' He shuddered, and she wondered if he was ever going to look at her again.

For the first time in years she wished Tyler were here. Damn him! Had he ever been there when she needed him?

'He made me wait in his boat. He wouldn't let me go home. He said he would turn me over to my dad.' His voice was trembling, the words stumbling out in a rush.

'He asked where my parents were, and I told him you were out flying.'

Mountain Man had interpreted that to mean that she was partying, having a good time, neglecting her son. She hoped he would leave soon. He was probably only here for supplies, and he would be gone. Meanwhile, she had the problem of trying to supervise a fourteen-year-old boy on summer holidays while she worked.

She slept fitfully that night, waking to the knowledge that she could not fly away and leave him to his own devices.

'Wake up, Shane! We're going flying!'

He stumbled out of his cabin, looking sleepy and about ten years old, except for the tallness that did not belong to a child. 'What d'ya mean?' He rubbed his eyes, watching as she put the kettle on the gas stove and sliced bread for the toaster.

'You're going with me.' She made her voice flat, hoping to avoid argument. 'I'm flying the sked to Rupert today, then a charter out to Englefield bay.' She shrugged. 'I suppose there may be other flights, too. This time of year, there's always someone comes along at the last minute wanting to go somewhere.'

'I don't want to go.' He picked up a piece of bread and started chewing on it.

A noise had been pulsing in the background for five minutes or so, low and unidentified. Now it came louder, the invasive pounding of an orchestra pulsing over *Island Wanderer*. She rubbed her forehead and tried to tune it out.

'You have no choice, Shane.' She caught two pieces of hot toast as they popped out of the toaster and started buttering them. 'You want jam on this? Yes? Shane, when you break the law, you lose your freedom. People go to jail for stealing.'

He watched her spread jam on the toast. 'Mom, it was only a couple of bucks. I coulda bought it. I had the money.'

'Well then, why didn't you? Are you crazy, Shane? Don't you realise that if they'd called the police you could have been charged, could have gone to jail?'

He shook his head. 'I wouldn't. The first offence, they don't do anything if you're a young offender. They—it's true, Mom! They just take you to your parents and tell them. Then if they get you a second time they—— Then they sometimes charge you. But they don't send fourteen-year-old kids to jail.'

What was her son doing with knowledge like this? What did the boys do when they were sitting on the wharf, talking? Is this what they talked about? Stealing and getting away with it? Who was playing that horrible music? Listening, feeling the headache coming, she felt as if Mrs Bentham were descending, about to come around a corner and confront her.

Tyler had always insisted, 'You've got to call her *Mother*. It's embarrassing in front of other people when you call her *Mrs Bentham*.'

Other people. Always other people. The right clothes and the right friends and the right music. She stared down at the denim covering her legs, and the music pounded in her mind, oppressive and painful.

What had she been saying? What had Shane said?

'Shane, you can't think like that. If you think it doesn't matter, you'll end up—— My God! You could end up in jail! You—— Why——' Her voice was threatening to rise out of control and she had to keep cool, had to think, not to react wildly. It was that damned music pounding and pounding, surging with the power of forty-seven or a hundred instruments. 'Next time,' she said grimly, 'if you have to have something, you buy it! You go to the counter and give it to the clerk, and you *pay*.'

He devoured the jam and toast in mere seconds, mumbling, 'How can I? They don't let kids buy those kinds of magazines. Brady tried and they wouldn't sell it to him. Harry's dad collects them, but he caught Harry with one and beat the tar out of him.'

'What is this?' she demanded. 'A club of voyeurs? What happened to Dungeons and Dragons?' Why hadn't she kept a closer eye on what he was doing in his leisure time? They were all fourteen and fifteen. Harry's voice had changed just recently, and Brady was sometimes shaving. If they were all looking at magazines like the one in the boat next door, what was she supposed to do or say? The only thing that was clear to her was that there had been stealing, and she had to put a stop to that.

'You're going to spend the summer with me,' she said, thinking of details and hoping she could swing it, that Luke would not mind too much. 'You're flying with me, and when you're not flying you'll be helping out at QC, helping Barry or Luke. Whatever there is for you to do.'

'A job?' His eyes brightened.

She said coldly, 'Do you think you deserve a job? Do you think I can recommend you to my boss as a trustworthy employee?'

She saw how her words hurt him, but she had to say them. He must understand, must learn.

She pushed back the main hatch and climbed out into the cockpit. The noise focused then, a full orchestra belting out one of Mrs Bentham's favourites. Mountain Man was standing in his cockpit, doing something to what looked like an artist's canvas on an easel.

So that was what he was, a penniless artist bumming around the province in a boat. A man who thought he had his own special artistic view of the world, who thought he was always right. He was quick enough to criticise her as a mother, to——

It was the music. Five more minutes of it and she would be insane, screaming wild and shattered into little pieces.

'Would you mind——?' He didn't hear anything. His eyes were on the shore, and he was doing something, making something take shape on the canvas. He was not painting. Sketching, she supposed, directly on to the canvas.

'Hey! Would you mind turning that noise down?'

He had to have heard her, but he kept moving his hand against the canvas, leaving behind a line that looked like the hill over there. How could you characterise a whole hill with one line?

'Turn that bloody racket off!'

His hand softly caressed another shape on to the canvas. The shopping centre, nestled against the hillside like a guest in the wilderness. When the shopping centre was at home with the hill, he turned to look at her, his eyes rather cold over the ragged beard.

'How on earth can you sail with a mess like that inside?' She had not meant to ask, but she could see it all through the window, and she did not want to talk about the strangely powerful lines on the canvas.

'Is that what you came to talk about?'

She swung her hair back, looked away, suddenly feeling too close to him. She wished she had tied her hair back for flying before she came up. That always made her feel a little more in control. 'No, I—— Would you please turn off that music?'

He stared at her as if he would be able to draw her on one of those canvases from memory, although the picture would not be one she would want to see.

'Why?' he asked.

'Why what?'

He snorted, said, 'Why should I turn off the music?'

She stepped away from him, came up against the side of her own cockpit. What was it about this man that irritated her so? She had been holding her temper for years, and it was as if it had all started boiling up on her the moment he sailed into this harbour.

'For heaven's sake! It's a terrible racket! I've been listening to it all morning, and I can't stand another minute of it!' She *never* screamed! She could hear Shane rushing from below, convinced something terrible was happening.

Mountain Man turned back to the easel, said, 'It's Dvořák, and it's probably time you learned to appreciate good music.'

He tuned her out, then, as if she had already gone. She stood for a long moment, staring at him, feeling more enraged than she could remember being in her whole life, yet horribly helpless. She felt like a small child wanting to throw a tantrum. She wanted to stomp over and pull his long hair, push the damned canvas over, anything to force him to pay attention to her, not ignore her as if she were nothing, nobody!

She turned and went down inside the boat, past Shane who was saying, 'Mom? You OK?' She nodded because she could not talk, and he said, 'What happened?'

She shook her head. The music. The man. Worrying about Shane. He was waiting for something, so she said, 'He's a very irritating man. He made me angry.'

Shane, surprisingly, looked disapproving, as if he felt she were at fault.

She turned away. 'Let's go. I've got to get to work.'

Half an hour later, she left Shane in the coffee lounge at QC Air and went down to the seaplane float to find her boss.

'Luke?'

He grunted, acknowledging her presence, his eyes on the Cessna's float, his broad hands touching the metal as if he could feel the weakness that might be there.

She pulled her soft cap down over her hair. 'Luke, do you mind if I take Shane along with me on the sked?'

He shook his head, frowning at the float. 'Why should I mind, Nick? You've done it before. We're going to have to get this rebuilt before we can trust it again.'

'It doesn't look all that bad.' She crouched down beside him, then saw what he had seen, the signs of structural damage inside. 'I wondered if I could take him along whenever there's room. It's summer, and he's at a bit of a loose end.'

He rocked back on his heels, watching her speculatively. 'Problems, Nick?'

'No, I—— Yes, I—I wanted to keep him busy, keep an eye on him. I wondered if you could dream up some jobs he could do around here? You don't need to pay him, but——'

He stood up and brushed off his trousers where he had been kneeling on the float. He had the kind of hair that did not show the greying because of its sun-bleached fairness. He was a broad man, husky and solid, not tall. Nicole was as tall as he was.

She had always liked him, but she kept a reserve between herself and everyone but Shane.

'Don't you think you should tell me what happened?' He pulled a rag out of his back pocket and rubbed at the dirt on his hands. 'After all, you're asking me to give him a job.'

'I don't want you to pay him.' This was not the time to give Shane rewards. It was time for punishment and restrictions.

'What did he do, Nick?'

She blurted, 'He stole a *Playboy* magazine from the store. I—no one knows about it. The captain of one of the transient sail-boats caught him. He—Luke, it's not funny!'

Her boss shook his head, a half-smile still on his face. 'Come on, Nick! I know it's serious, the stealing part. But has he ever taken anything before?'

'I don't think so.' She hoped not.

'Well, how else was he to get it? Nick, the kid's how old? Fifteen?'

'Fourteen.'

Luke nodded. 'All hormones and frustration, wanting to know what it's all about and—— Well, he's got no man around. He can hardly ask his mother, can he? Don't look like that, Nick. It's no particular inadequacy in you, except that you're a woman.'

'Thanks a lot!' She stepped away, tried to bring her voice to its usual cool tones. 'Luke, I—this scares the hell out of me. Do you really think it's just—that it's natural?'

'Oh, it's natural enough, but of course you're right to be concerned. You can't just let the stealing pass, although he'd probably have bought the magazine if the store would sell it to him.'

'That's what he said. But I want to keep him busy.'

'Best thing you can do, Nick. It's a dangerous time.' He grinned, said, 'You're probably wondering where I get off talking like an expert. I don't have any kids, but I remember that as one of the worst stages of my life. It's an easy time for a kid to get into trouble. Let him do some real work, get paid for it. That'll make him feel good about himself, give him some self-esteem.'

'Shane has loads of self-esteem. He's a very——'

Luke grinned and she realised that she had been sounding like a typical aroused parent defending her child. Johnny can do no wrong. Luke insisted, 'Nick, no kid has enough self-esteem at that age. He may act like it, but believe me—— Is he up at the office? OK, I'll talk to him. We'll put him to work. I'll pay him, but you can be sure it won't be a cent more than he's worth. I've been needing someone for odd jobs around here. Barry's getting too busy in the office.'

Beneath his gruff exterior, Luke was considerate and thoughtful. She thought Laurie Lucas was a lucky lady to have this man for a husband, and it was one time when she was relieved to hand over a little of the responsibility to a man.

The days passed and Nicole started to breathe a little easier. She was sure the job was the thing that made Shane accept the restrictions, the humiliating situation of being unable to see his friends, and having to accompany his mother on her flights.

She didn't talk to Mountain Man at all. He was around. She saw the back of his shaggy head as he walked away on the shore, the beard as he stood in his cockpit and painted.

'He's a painter,' said Shane with awe on the third day he was tied up to them.

Nicole shrugged away the look of worship in Shane's eyes. 'You'll be taking art next year.'

He said bitterly, 'I've been taking art for years. Every year I take it, and——'

'I know, Shane, but it's such a small town, such a small school. You'll have private lessons next year, and a good art instructor.'

Had she been wrong to keep him on the islands these last six years? She had fought his grandmother every step of the way over this issue. Surely he hadn't missed that much? He had been happy, and doing well in school. She would not have let him go even now, except for the testing that had been done this year, the UBC team who had told her that Shane was far too gifted artistically and intellectually for the school to cope with, that he should go to a school that could offer special courses, special programmes.

Seven more weeks and he would be gone. She hoped Mountain Man would not spend all seven weeks tied to them, playing Dvořák every time he picked up a paint-brush. If he did, she would be insane by summer's end. She was starting to hear the music even when it was not there. The only time she seemed to be able to escape it was when she was flying.

Then, one day, she and Shane came home from the seaplane base and found the wooden boat gone. She felt free, as if an oppression had been lifted. Silence, only the sounds that belonged. People walking past. Boats mooring. Life returned to normal.

Nicole was stranded by fog on Lyell Island one night. Luke assured her on the radio that he and Laurie would take Shane for the night. After that, Shane had standing instructions to go to Luke's house whenever his mother was late.

July melted away. Nicole felt panic-stricken by the knowledge that half of her precious summer with her son was gone already, but Luke had agreed that she could be free the last two weeks of August. She would take Shane sailing, try to regain the closeness they used to have. The job was the best thing that had happened for Shane this summer, but he seemed to be growing more and more distant from her.

She hated having to fly late, but the days were long and people were wanting to go everywhere—to mines, to archaeological digs, to Indian villages, to logging camps.

On the last evening of July she returned from a charter to Masset and unloaded three passengers on the wharf. Shane had met the plane, tying the pontoons to the wharf and preparing to refuel it.

Luke came down behind him. 'Nick, would you mind taking the Cessna over to Security Cove before you quit?' She could hardly say no. All winter she would be flying only a few hours each day. Luke said, 'We'll give Shane supper.'

'What is it, Luke? How many people?'

'Cargo, not people,' said Luke. 'Delicate and important, but I don't know how much. A Cessna would do, he said.'

So she took the small plane on her own, circling high over Queen Charlotte, then letting the Cessna glide west with the power low. She loved the feel of the Cessna, although it was smaller than the Beaver and far slower than the twin-engine Goose. For her, flying it had a special excitement, warm memories.

She checked her chart, wondering what this Mr Kealy was doing anchored on the wild west coast of the Charlottes. What was his urgent, fragile cargo?

She circled over the cove, spotting the solitary boat swinging at anchor right in the middle. It was a sailboat, its mast appearing shortened because of her height. It would have been better if it were a power-boat, no wires and masts to get her wings tangled in when she tried to get close.

She circled out towards the sea, then cut the engines back as the flaps went on. She made a perfect touchdown on the glassy water of the inlet, then used the ribbon of water like a road that took her straight to the centre of Security Cove, taxiing easily. She wanted to get home to her son, but she was not rushing.

She cut the Cessna's engine when she was comfortably close to the boat. Then, for the first time, she took a good look at the boat itself from the water level.

Why her? Why couldn't Luke have flown this one? Damn! It would be Mountain Man himself!

She gritted her teeth and undid her seat-belt, then opened her door and stepped out on to the pontoon. He was on the deck of his boat, watching the plane, and he still hadn't found a razor or a barber.

His voice was clear and friendly, and he obviously did not recognise her with her hair tied back and the cap pulled down to shade her eyes from the sun. 'How do you want to do this? I've got twenty canvases to transfer. They're tied up in bundles of five. The biggest is three feet square.'

She frowned, her eyes settling on the dinghy on the deck of the sail-boat. It was a small inflatable, not the sort of thing for this job. She tipped her head back to eye the rigging of the sail-boat, looking for a place she could swing her wing over to let the plane get close enough.

'Sail-boats are terrible for seaplane rendezvous,' she called across to him. She saw him start as her voice carried, but did not let him see that she noticed. With the jean jacket and the cap, she could be a slender man at a distance. She didn't know if he recognised her yet, but he knew that she was a woman, and women pilots were unusual.

'You've got two choices,' she told him, her voice businesslike. She freed the paddle and manoeuvred the Cessna closer, nose towards him. 'You can load your dinghy and bring the stuff to me, or I can bring the

Cessna's nose in and we can secure it against your boat long enough to make the transfer. You can pass things down to me from the deck.'

He frowned. She understood his reservations. Either way, it meant passing his canvases to her while she stood on the pontoons. She said, 'It's up to you, but if I were you I'd go for the plane against your boat. That's one transfer instead of two, and you'll be on a stable platform when you're handing me things. If you've got ropes around the bundles so I can hang on to something, I think it will go all right.' If Mountain Man would only follow her instructions.

'Makes sense. What do you want me to do?' He was eyeing the plane and his boat, seeming to appreciate the difficulty of the whole operation.

'You've never done this before, have you?'

He shook his head. 'Never. And I hadn't realised how long those wings are.'

She paddled closer. 'Catch my propeller as it comes up to you, but for heaven's sake, don't let it turn! Just hold it. Let me do the manoeuvring.'

She had to admit that he was good. He did exactly what she said, and he had the sense to have lines ready, and to let her decide where she wanted them. Within ten minutes she had the Cessna secure enough that she could feel good about the transfer.

'OK,' she announced, careful to keep her footing solid on the pontoons.

'Well——' He glanced back at the bundles of canvases that were stacked in his cockpit, then he went and picked up the first one, but looked distinctly uneasy as he handed it down to her. 'Have you got it? Don't drop it in the water, for God's sake!'

'I won't.' She was a little amused to find that he was actually human, although it did not show in her cool voice. 'I'm always very careful.'

His brows went up, as if he doubted that, and of course he had recognised her and he was worried about his precious paintings. She wrapped the twine firmly around her wrist, then moved carefully along the pontoon to the door, using her free hand to grasp the wing-strut solidly. She had left the door open and she reached and deposited the package securely inside.

'I'll put them in the back seat,' she told him as she walked back for the next parcel. 'Then I can fasten a seat-belt around them.'

'Are you expecting turbulence?' He frowned. Her first impression had been right. This was not a man anyone would want to have as an enemy. He was not quite civilised.

'No.' She tucked a stray hair under the cap. 'I'm just being careful. That's what I'm paid for. Are you going to give me the next bundle?'

She held her hands out and he surrendered the bundle. He was definitely tense, and she hoped nothing terrible would happen, because he was not going to be at all understanding if she dropped five canvases into the Pacific Ocean.

He relaxed when the transfer was done, but he still was not smiling. 'You'll fasten them?'

'Yes.' She concealed her irritation, jerked her head in a gesture towards the blue sky. 'There's not going to be any turbulence. Winds are steady up there.'

'You're heading straight into Queen Charlotte? Not making any other stops? I don't want those paintings being ferried all over the islands.'

This was getting to be a bit too much. She said slowly and too patiently, 'I'm taking off in five minutes precisely, and I'll be landing in Queen Charlotte in twenty minutes, maybe a little more. The water's calm here, and there. I'll take your precious artwork and lock it in the office until the taxi comes to take it to the airport at Sandspit in the morning.' Her voice developed a bite as he kept frowning, staring at her. 'You're in more danger from the taxi driver loading it than you are from me. Believe it or not, Mr Kealy, I'm the smoothest pilot around this area. Cool. No hot rodding. They give me all the phobia cases, because I don't take chances.'

If she could see anything through that damned mess of hair, she thought it would be anger. He growled, 'Just don't take any chances with those paintings. I don't give a damn about your phobia cases. Those canvases are fragile, not frightened.'

The man was impossible! She released his lines from the pontoons. She was not about to ask him to do anything, but he did it anyway, holding the propeller to steady the aeroplane until she had the paddle out.

She turned the plane and paddled away from his boat. *Charmaine*, it was called. Who was Charmaine? His girlfriend? His wife? She had not been able to read the name when the boat had been tied to *Island Wanderer* in Queen Charlotte, but it was plain on the bows when she looked back from the pontoon of the seaplane.

He was standing, watching her, the beard not hiding the fact that he did not think much of her. She decided unwillingly that he was a good-looking man, despite the fact that he badly needed a shave and a haircut.

She wondered what arrangements he had made about paying for this pick-up, but Luke had not asked her to collect any money, and she was not about to confront him on any issues if she could avoid it.

She climbed in and fastened his bundles with the seat-belts, looping them through the twine that held the paintings. He had the whole thing covered with cardboard, quite securely packed, so there was nothing to see but cardboard, twine, and the delivery instructions. Lyndon Boydon, *Boydon Galleries*. The address was a Vancouver one, and she had a feeling she had heard of the galleries. So he might be a successful painter, or at least one who sometimes sold. She shrugged. Whichever, he was a bad-tempered artist.

She did her pre-flight inspection, then climbed in and belted herself in. He was going to watch until she was out of sight. Unnerving.

Damn it! It was more than unnerving. The man was a pain, an irritation. Critical of everything. Her son. Herself as a mother. Her abilities as a pilot. When did he stop judging other people? He was a mess, unshaven and unkempt. His boat was a disaster area of paints and turpentine, canvases and brushes.

The engine fired at once and she idled, turning the seaplane in the water. When she was turned sideways to the boat, looking out the side window at him, she swung open the door and shouted, 'Some day you should have a shave! It might make you look a little less like some wild man down from the mountains!'

Over the engine noise she could not hear if he answered, but her voice would have carried well to him. She was grinning as she turned and started a slow taxi away from *Charmaine* and her captain. The man was definitely bad for her. She was not the kind of person who made nasty comments like that, but being around him made her want to shout and throw things.

She pushed the cap off her head and tried to rake her hair back with her fingers, but the long strands were already pulled back and all she did was yank some of them out. This was no way to fly a plane, half angry and half laughing, her heart pounding for no reason at all.

Breathe deeply. Calm down. She settled back in the seat, checked her seat-belt, put the headphones on. She didn't call in to the base on the radio. The hill would make this a dead spot for radio contact to Queen Charlotte. She would check in when she was airborne.

Charmaine was several hundred feet away by now. The distance helped her feel calmer. If she had any control over events, this would be the last time she saw Mountain Man Kealy. Too damned arrogant. Too bad-tempered. He was certainly not her kind of man.

Tyler had not been her kind of man either, although he had been as different from this rough artist as it was possible to be. She shook her head, upset by the way her thoughts were going. She did *not* want to know what that beard would feel like against her cheek. She did not give a damn whether Mountain Man had a girlfriend named Charmaine!

She turned and started back towards the cove, gaining speed. There was plenty of room to take off now. She opened the throttle and let the Cessna eat up the water, gaining speed and straining to lift, approaching the sail-boat fast. Still on the water, she switched the magneto selector first to the left mag, then the right. Many pilots would skip this routine test on the return leg of a quick turnaround flight like this. She never had.

Both mags tested good. She switched the selector to BOTH, then let the Cessna fly itself off the water, lifting, rising, sweeping up, the throttle wide and the engine developing the surge of power that was needed to climb above the hills.

She glanced down and saw the beautiful curve of the boat shrinking against the water, the man standing on the deck, looking up with his hand shading his eyes from the sun low on the horizon. She felt an inexplicable pang, a tightening in her throat as if she had to hold back tears.

She watched the trees dropping, the altimeter recording her ascent. Two hundred and fifty feet. Three hundred. Soon she would start to bank, making the turn towards Queen Charlotte. She——

Abruptly, the engine noise changed. Her eyes flew back to the console. Something was wrong. She had lost a hundred RPM. The climb was slower. She had to ease the nose down and let the Cessna rise more gently.

Four hundred feet now, finally. She needed another hundred feet before she could safely do anything. Her heart was beating a little faster, adrenalin pumping through her veins. She felt sharp and alert, and ready to react if this turned into more than a routine problem.

Almost four hundred and fifty feet. Not long now. She called her base station on the radio as she waited... Five hundred feet. She switched to the right mag, keeping her hand on the switch, ready to change quickly if she had to... No, the right was OK. The engine roared on. She switched to the left.

Silence. The engine stopped, the Cessna slowing, starting to drop.

Nicole instantly threw the switch back to the right and adjusted the nose down. She couldn't have said which she did first. Both were automatic. The engine roared to life again.

Luke's voice crackled in her ears. She brought the nose up gently, slowly climbing back to five hundred feet as she spoke. 'Luke, I've just taken off from Security Cove. I've got one mag out. Must be an intermittent. They tested OK on take-off—I'm circling to go back in.' She banked gently.

Luke was saying, 'We'll be losing our light soon. I'm afraid you're stuck until daylight. Good thing there's someone in there. You should be able to beg a berth.'

Ask Mountain Man to give her a place to sleep? She gritted her teeth and concentrated on the flying, heard Luke say, 'I'm taking off at daybreak. I'll drop you off a replacement magneto on my way out.'

'Luke, could you take Shane overnight?' She did not want him alone, at a loose end.

'No problem, Nick. Don't worry about him. We'll look after him until you're back. I'll take him with me on the flight tomorrow, too. I could use someone to help pack and carry.'

Thank God for Luke! He understood, did not consider her obligations to Shane as a barrier to her working as a pilot. Without Luke's understanding, his willingness to give her a chance at this job, she would have had to go begging for work. Flying was the only marketable skill she had.

She made a perfect landing, coming to rest on the other side of the bay from Mountain Man's boat. Of course he would be watching, damn him!

She climbed out on to the pontoon and lifted the engine cover. There it was! The wire leading from the left magneto was damaged, shorting on the fire wall. It would be easy to fix. She would not need the spare mag Luke was bringing, just a bit of electrical tape. There was bound to be some in the plane. If not, *he* would probably have some on his boat.

Repairing the wire would not get her out of here tonight. Damn and double damn! The light was going. There was simply not enough time. She pulled the cover back across the engine, feeling a sick dread.

What was it about the man? He made her feel exposed, as if he could see all her failures, her inadequacies.

She was a success, damn it! Making a living doing something she loved, supporting the son she loved. Why did he make her feel as if she should be something else, something more? Why must she feel this sick inadequacy that brought back all the years with Tyler and his mother?

She closed the engine cover. The current had drifted her towards *Charmaine*, but she was far enough away to anchor and have room to swing.

She could see him, moving on deck, launching his dinghy. He would be cold-eyed, scornful. He would probably believe this was her fault, that something about her being female had messed up the damned magneto! He would not know about the plane, the magnetos, because he obviously was not a pilot. That wouldn't matter. He would not know a magneto from a legal contract, but he would simply believe she was to blame, without caring why.

Legal contract? Why was she doing that? Why keep comparing him to Tyler, as if——

Damn! Why her? Why wasn't she a daring pilot? If she were, she might have tried flying back. After all, what were the chances of the second mag going in the space of fifteen minutes? Then she would have been safe in her own bed, not stranded here with her lips passing words she had heard in logging camps.

She *never* swore. It was *him* doing this to her, making her feel uncertain and defensive, even bringing profanities to her lips.

The word that echoed around the cabin of the small seaplane was one that she had slapped Shane for saying last month.

CHAPTER THREE

'WHAT happened?' He tied his dinghy to the cleat on the Cessna's pontoon. 'I heard the engine stop just after you took off.'

She shrugged, not looking up from lowering the anchor. 'Nothing serious. One of the mags is out.' He would not have a clue what she was talking about, but she did not care.

'Aren't you supposed to check them before you take off?' the hateful man demanded.

She gritted her teeth. She would *not* look at him. His long jeans-clad legs as he stood in the dinghy were enough. 'I checked them while I was getting her up on the step. They were fine. After take-off one cut out—the shield wore off the electrical wire.' Damn! Why was she explaining, defending herself to him?

'I've got some electrical tape.' His voice was neutral. 'I could probably fix it for you.'

The anchor bit into the mud bottom below. She felt the plane start to swing gently as the rope came tight. She glared across the front of the plane at him, bit out, '*I* can fix it, but the light's going. I can't take off again now until morning. If I were incompetent, as you seem to think I am, I would have taken a chance on the other mag and flown home! Then I'd be in my own bed tonight, and I wouldn't have to put up with any more of your company!'

She was breathless, heart pounding, and she was furious, blazing mad! He was getting angry, too. She could see it in the still paleness of those blue eyes. She should shut up, but she jerked at the soft visor of her cap, and said tightly, 'Since we're into unwanted advice here—it seems to come naturally to you, telling other people what to do—has anyone ever told you that it's a bad idea to stand up in a small boat? You might fall in.' She would love that, seeing him dumped in the cold water.

'Listen, lady—whatever the hell your name is. I probably shouldn't call you *lady*, because that's one thing you're *not*.' His scornful voice bewildered her. 'If you want to scream and argue, you can do it on your own. I came over here to find out if you needed help—and to make damned sure that my paintings didn't come to any grief.'

'Oh, for—your bloody paintings will be fine. They're securely wrapped, inside the plane. Will you at least give me credit for knowing my job? I've ferried all sorts of fragile cargo all over these islands. Your paintings will make it, unscarred!'

He pushed a paint-spattered hand through unruly long hair. 'I don't know if you know your job, but you've got problems with the rest of life. With an attitude like yours, I've got to wonder how you managed to get yourself a man for long enough to have a kid! Whoever the crazy man is, I can sure as hell understand why he's not still around!'

She jerked as if he had struck her, her hand clenching on the strut of the Cessna to keep her balance, her throat seizing up and making the words almost impossible. 'Sure, bring a man into it! After all, what's a woman without a man? That's what it comes down to, isn't it, Mountain Man?'

His eyes had narrowed. He was watching as if she were a specimen that had just done something interesting. She felt a horrible conviction that he was seeing things no one was allowed to see. Defensive fury welled up in her voice.

'Typical macho male response! A woman says something you don't like, and you tell her she's not attractive to men! Big deal! Take a look at yourself! Mountain Man Kealy! Big man, all hairy surliness. You don't give a damn about anyone but yourself! You're hiding out in the wilderness, can't take society. Or is it that society can't take you? If we're going to talk about getting a mate, no woman would have you if you were the last man on these islands!'

Sounds echoed around the cove, fragments of her shouted words. What was she saying? What was she doing? She yanked the cap off and pulled at the tie in her hair. Hair tumbled everywhere, covering her face, her neck, the heated flush that was not Nicole Bentham. Wow! This man sure knew how to push her buttons. She had never been so angry with anyone.

The sun was almost gone, a flaming red to the west. There were low, fair-weather clouds creeping in from the sea, all red and hot. Even the water around them was glowing with a red depth that spread up the hillside behind.

He was watching, saying nothing, as if she were some kind of side show. She turned away from him and pulled open the door on the passenger side.

She mumbled, 'I'm sorry. I don't know what got into me.' She leaned into the door, busied herself checking his cargo, mainly to get out of his sight. Her hair was all over, getting in her way as she lay half in and half out of the plane. That was the reason she always kept it tied back, that and the fact that her sex was a little less obvious.

She felt the plane shift in the water. He had stepped on to the pontoon. She called, 'I don't need any help, thanks. You can go on back to your boat. I'll be fine.'

The door on the other side swung open. 'Get your things together and I'll take you back to the boat for the night.'

'I'm fine here.' There was no way on this earth that she was going to sleep on his boat. Charmaine, whoever she was, could have him.

'That's ridiculous! Where are you going to sleep?' He stood on the strut and swung into the pilot's seat, twisting to glare at her.

She straightened and stared across the passenger seat at him. 'I'll sleep right where you are.'

He snorted. 'And freeze to death! That jacket will seem pretty thin by the time night is over. It's a clear night, and it'll be cold.' His voice told her that he knew he had right on his side.

She turned and ducked around to the other side, passing the open door near him as quickly as she could, heading for the luggage compartment, saying, 'I've got a sleeping-bag in the luggage compartment. It's getting dark. You'd better go back.' She opened the compartment and took out two empty plastic jerry cans.

'That's ridiculous!' He slid out of her seat, stood only inches away from her. He was so damned tall. She had been able to look Tyler almost straight in the eye, but this man made her tip her head back, made her feel small and helpless.

'It's not ridiculous at all,' she insisted stubbornly. 'I've done it before.' She gripped the lower strut as she bent down to fill a jerry can with water. She was feeling more in control now, her voice almost cool. 'It's quite simple, Mr Kealy. I'll get the sleeping-bag, put it in the front, curl up and sleep.' Simple, yes, but horribly uncomfortable. She would sleep poorly, wake stiff and aching.

She twisted to glance up at him, her lips half smiling because he really was looking a bit at a loss, as if he did not know what to do about her. She had no need to feel nervous. This man might be scornful and bossy, but he was not the kind to try forcibly hauling her over to the boat.

Her eyes lit with laughter as she thought of him trying. He might be taller, stronger, but she could guarantee to dump the dinghy and land them both in the water before she would let him force her anywhere!

'Who are you?' His voice was sharp, disturbed. 'I've seen you somewhere before, haven't I?'

She swallowed. What had reminded him? She lifted the heavy jerry can slightly and twisted the lid on it. After all these years, surely no one would clearly remember a newspaper picture?

She could see that it was bothering him. He crouched down, the denim of his jeans pulling tight across muscular thighs, his long-fingered hands grasping the red hand-hold of the can. 'I'll lift that up for you. It's heavy. What are you doing with it, anyway?'

She shook her head, tying a length of rope to the handle. 'It can stay in the water. I'm just tying it to the wing. Then, if it gets windy in here, the Cessna won't be tempted to take flight.' She was talking casually, but he was still watching and she did not want him to remember where he had seen her. He was trouble enough to her as it was, without knowing all about her past and her failures.

'Where have I seen you before?' He was not going to give up. It would worry at him until he placed her.

She managed to throw him an impatient glance. 'I've never seen you before in my life, Mr Kealy. I assure you, I would remember.'

He was not satisfied. 'Your hair...your face—I thought I recognised you back at Queen Charlotte City, but then——' His eyes were narrowed, watching her. She stood up, fastening the rope to the underside of the wing and drawing it tight until the heavy container of water was hanging heavy, yet still floating in the water.

She picked up the second can. 'Would you mind getting out of my way? I've got to get to the other side.' Slipping past him was not something she wanted to do, but there was no choice.

His arm brushed against her like a high-voltage obstacle, making her stumble. He caught her quickly, grabbing for her and the strut overhead at the same time. She was caught tight against his chest, her breasts squashed flat against him. She twisted, but her feet found only water for a hold. The movement brought them into intimate contact and he gritted, 'For God's sake, hold still or I'll drop you!'

Then she was free, her wet running shoes planted firmly on the pontoon. She stepped back, averting her eyes, turning to move away. He saw too damned much, but his cool eyes gave nothing away. His body had, though. When he held her roughly against him, she had felt every ridge of his chest and his thighs, and she had felt the quick, hard evidence of his arousal.

That was what had her breathless, her heart pounding. She was in the middle of nowhere, trapped with a man who did not like her, but desired her. Would he ever go back to his boat and leave her alone?

His low voice said, 'I can tell you one thing. I've never had you in my arms before. I would remember that.'

She stared at the water flowing into the open spout of the jerry can. It was swirling, making a pattern like sink water going down the drain. Her voice sounded like gravel. 'You don't know me from anywhere. The world is full of blondes. You've mistaken me for another woman.'

Thankfully, she could not see him. There was just his voice. 'What's your name?'

Nicole Bentham. No way she was telling him that. If he could not quite remember the face, the name might give him the answer he was after.

'Do you have a name?'

She said shortly, 'Nick.'

She heard the door to the luggage compartment, saw his legs moving under the belly of the plane. Nervously, she demanded, 'What are you doing?'

'Getting out your sleeping-bag.' Was he laughing? 'You'll want it to keep you warm.' His legs strode forward along the far pontoon.

She liked his legs. Long and lean and hard. She had tried to label him as an unwashed heathen, but a moment ago she had smelled clean, hard male; an erotic, natural scent that had stirred something primitive inside her.

She did not want to feel like that. Not for any man, especially not for this one. 'Where are you taking my sleeping-bag?' The panic was in her voice as she saw her bag drop into his dinghy.

He said quietly, soothing, 'Your anchor seems to be holding. Once you've got those weights on the wings arranged to your satisfaction, there's no reason why you can't leave the plane here for the night.'

She was not sure if she could handle a night in such close quarters with this shaggy man. Sleeping on the same boat, hearing him breathe, the sound of him turning in his sleep. Why did he get under her skin? His music...his arrogance...the man himself?

She fussed over the rope. The sun had set, the red had flowed into a deep darkness surrounded by low hills, untouched evergreen trees stretching to a sky whose blueness had faded to grey. He was waiting in the dinghy. Soon he would be telling her it was time to go before dark fell.

She walked out to the end of the pontoon, pushed her hands into the pockets of her jacket, shivering already. That was the trouble with these clear summer days. The sun turned the islands into an incredibly painful beauty. Then night came, no clouds to hold the heat in, frigid water all around. Even with the sleeping-bag she would be uncomfortably cold.

He was not a man who talked a lot. Quiet, watching, and when he had something to say it was usually unpleasant and to the point. She wished she had kept her cap on, her hair tied back. His eyes kept losing themselves in her hair. There was nothing special about it, long and blonde and straight, except that it was exactly the kind of hair Tyler Bentham's wife had.

She managed an impersonal, 'Mr Kealy, I'd appreciate it if you would hand me my sleeping-bag and head on back to your boat before it's dark.' She shifted her feet carefully to avoid losing her balance. 'Thank you for your offer of a berth on your boat.' He hadn't offered, but it had been implied. She shook her hair away from her face. 'I'd rather stay here for the night.'

He untied the line to the dinghy. For a moment she thought he was going to leave with her sleeping-bag. She wanted him gone, at almost any cost, but she did not want to die of hypothermia sleeping uncovered in an unheated plane on a cold night.

'My bag——'

He jockeyed the dinghy around, brought the rubber tube bumping against the pontoon beside her. He shipped the close oar and grasped the cleat on the top of the pontoon. He was floating just at her feet. There was nowhere to look but down at the man, and he was watching her, something dangerously quiet in his eyes, one elbow resting on his outthrust knee.

If it were Tyler, he would jump up and stand on the pontoon, draw himself up and make sure she knew who was taller. Mountain Man didn't seem to care who was looking down at who.

'Look here.' His voice was cool, horribly reasonable. 'I know you're not exactly enamoured of me, but just because we don't like each other much—if you sleep out here you'll be miserable by morning. Your feet are wet, and if you don't come over to *Charmaine* and put your shoes and socks at the fire, they'll stay wet. By morning, you'd be out cold from hypothermia, and I can't fly that plane out of here.'

She bit her lip uncertainly. A boat was such close quarters. He seemed to read her mind. 'If you're worried that I might take advantage of the situation, you needn't.'

She flushed, said hurriedly, 'I wasn't,' but it was only half true. His sexuality was certainly part of the problem, but it was her own awareness of it that bothered her. She had been alone enough years to have a good feel for the kind of man who would try to force himself on a woman. This man would not deign to take a woman who did not want him.

Even if he wanted her.

It was years since she had been that close to a man, held tight in his arms. This artist would never believe her, but only one man had ever held her that close, in such intimate contact, although she could never remember feeling such an uncomfortably sharp awareness of Tyler's sexuality. Was that because he was so much taller than Tyler, had made her feel almost tiny in his arms?

She felt the cold wetness of her feet. What did she have to dry herself with? 'All right,' she said, shuddering, and she climbed into the dinghy, feeling as if she were going to her own execution, looking past him, over his shoulder in the direction he rowed.

His boat was only a dark shadow against the sky as they slipped back across the water. As he pulled the oars, she could see the hard bulge of his biceps, even though she was not looking. The thinness was deceptive. This was a very strong man. In dress clothes, the muscles would be concealed by the lean length of him; in jeans and an old flannel shirt thin from hundreds of washings, he looked primitive.

When he stopped and held the dinghy for her, she hesitated, then shrugged and swung herself up on to his boat, holding his lifelines and feeling his eyes on her, watching the curve of her leg and her hip from below.

Why was she here? Was she insane?

He became businesslike when he arrived on the deck beside her. 'Get inside and get those wet things off. I'll find something for you.'

He disappeared into the boat, and she followed as far as the salon that was down two steps from the wheelhouse. This was where she had found Shane that day, but it was also where the stove was belting out warmth. She was tracking wet footprints all over his boat, but he wasn't much of a housekeeper anyway.

She sat on the settee near the fire and took off her wet shoes and socks. The legs of her jeans were wet, too, but she was not about to take *them* off. He emerged from the forward cabin, threw her a towel and a pair of thick woollen socks.

'The jeans, too,' he instructed abruptly, then disappeared again to emerge a moment later with a long grey pair of jogging pants. Then he turned and left her.

She could have been alone except for the clattering and banging that was coming from the wheelhouse. That might mean he was cooking, because the galley had been there on one side of the wheelhouse. She hoped he was. She had not had supper yet, and she had nothing with her, although there were emergency rations back in the Cessna.

She wished she had not come with him. She could have dried herself somehow, and she could have eaten without having to hope *he* would think to feed her.

With anyone else, she would simply say, 'Have you got something I could eat? I'm starving. A sandwich? Some toast? Anything!'

He seemed to be thoroughly involved out there, and there was no way he could see her unless he had X-ray vision. She shivered and unzipped her jeans, pulling the clinging wet denim away from her legs. They were wetter than she had thought, and she was all goose-bumps from the freezing water. She rubbed at her legs and feet with the towel, then pulled on the jogging pants. They were far too long, but the ankles were elastic. The socks were massive. He must have very large feet. She giggled, realising that although she had been very aware of his masculine shape, she had never looked down as far as his feet.

Lord, she was just as bad as Shane with his girlie magazines! Wondering what this man would look like without that shirt. Without those jeans. Maybe it was the isolation. She had been too long in the north, living on these islands that contained only a few people, people who wanted to live closer to the water and the trees than to civilisation.

It was dark outside now, dark in the salon, too. She heard a click and saw an echo of light from the wheelhouse. She was terribly tired. If she tried, she might manage to fall asleep without eating. She took her jacket off and curled up on the narrow settee near the stove, pulling the jacket over her shoulders and drawing her legs up to her abdomen for warmth.

She might never see him again once dawn came, but she thought she would probably never be able to pass an art gallery without going in and looking for any paintings by a man named Kealy.

He heated soup on the gas stove, sliced bread and cheese to go with it. He had not stopped to eat since lunch. It was likely that she had not had supper either, if she had been flying all day.

He remembered that first day in Queen Charlotte. He had felt drawn to the boy, sympathetic to his embarrassment at being caught with the magazine. It reminded him of an incident from his own teenage years.

The mother was another thing. When he saw her, blonde hair spread around her like a halo, he had thought that she fitted the boat. Beautiful, expensive, and untouchable. A lady of leisure, amusing herself, neglecting her child.

It had taken about two minutes for him to realise that she was something else, something more complex, and that he had seen her before. He had intended to sail away from the small village of Queen Charlotte almost at once, to buy some provisions and head for the remote west coast. But he had stayed for days, doubly caught—tied by the painting he had to finish, the village that was a part of these magic islands; and by the woman he remembered from somewhere.

It had become a challenge. He would not ask her, would not make any move to learn details that might give the answer away. He had just watched, disapproving because she was gone a lot, leaving early in the morning, dressed in jeans and thin shirts under that jacket, her hair flying around her and making a mockery of the masculine style of her dress, as did the enticing curve of her thigh and hip. The denim did nothing to hide the fact that she was all slender softness, lean and firm and silky smooth.

If she was on her way to work, she would be dressed in dresses and trouser suits—but you did not own a boat like *Island Wanderer* if you had to work for a living.

Unwillingly, he had started dreaming about her. He had never seen her without the jacket, but he could have drawn a nude that would make her wonder if he had been peeking in through her portholes.

It was too damned long since he had had a woman, but she was definitely not his kind. Where was the man she belonged to? Why was she here on the islands? Was she waiting for Shane's father? Did her coolness start burning when he was near? Or did she go out to other men?

Her face lay in his memory, elusive, the half-knowledge telling him that she was more than smooth innocence sheathing a passionate nature. A lady free with herself, not a lady at all. If he shaved and dressed in the clothes he had not worn in years, the suits and the ties, the expensive shoes—if he did that, she would turn soft and warm for him. That was the kind of woman she was. Anyone's woman, so long as he had money and polish.

She haunted his dreams. Hormones. Sex. A man too long without a woman. Whatever it was, it had not stopped until he left the town, taking to the wild coast and burying himself in his paintings, forgetting everything until noon today.

He had dropped his brush, exhausted, yet knowing the painting needed more work. He must rest first, regain his freshness. He had staggered over to the galley, disorientated by the world of dishes and hunger, his mind still in the magic of light on water, the mystery of a cabin deserted years ago, almost hidden in the trees.

He had picked up a loaf of bread and a knife. Then his eyes had fallen on his watch, lying abandoned on the counter, not worn in more than a week. Twelve-forty. That was irrelevant, but the date was important. The thirty-first of July. He had promised Lyndon, promised him faithfully, that he would deliver the paintings before the first of August. Lyndon had wanted more than the paintings.

'Just don't forget,' Lyndon had growled. 'Don't get lost in some damned inlet with your nose in a canvas and your mind in never-never land.'

He had laughed, but here he was and July was over, and Lyndon would be furious. Then, when he had turned on the radio, called the coastguard to try for a telephone patch, he had found that these hills shielded him from radio contact.

He had had to pull anchor and motor out for miles before he could get radio contact with the coast station. Finally, he was clear of the hills and he had managed to make a radio telephone call to a seaplane charter company in Queen Charlotte, making complicated arrangements that appeared to be mercifully commonplace to the man he talked to. Then he had made another call to Lyndon to reassure him.

He had got back into sheltered waters before too many things fell over. The easel had fallen and his box of paints scattered everywhere, but only one tube had not had its lid on, and the amber paint was hardly noticeable on the varnished floor once he'd used turpentine on it. Just a dullish spot where the turps had damaged the varnish.

He had bundled up all his dry canvases, taking them from the racks he had built in the after cabin and wrapping them first with plastic, then in the cardboard he kept for this purpose. Once that was done, he was free to get back to work. He turned on his stereo and set the half-finished painting back on the easel.

Shades of light and darkness in water. He moulded them, blended and contrasted, brush on canvas, paints swirled into God's colours on his palette.

When he stepped back and knew it was right, the sun was low in the sky, not setting yet, but his good light gone.

The seaplane had circled just as he cleaned his brushes. The charter company was good, giving him exactly what he had asked for. At the end of the day, not disturbing his work more than need be. He watched the landing. Seven years ago he had never once seen a seaplane close up. Now he was accustomed to them, flew in them when he had to go somewhere in the wilds quickly, and loved watching their flight.

The landing was very smooth, as if the pilot enjoyed the artistry of touching the pontoons very gently, very slowly on to the water. Funny, you could tell a lot about a person from watching him handle a car or a plane. There was something gentle about the way the small float plane taxied into the cove, the engine muted, nothing done in a hurry.

He was surprised when the denim leg popped out from the door, followed by an enticing curve. A woman, dressed in bush clothes but looking very feminine despite it. He liked the cap that was intended to shadow her face, hide the femininity. It had the allure of fine lingerie, tempting a man's hand to slide it away and discover what was underneath.

As she slid to her feet and turned, the motion caught at him and he knew who she was. Shane's mother. A bush pilot? Who was she?

He looked down on her from his deck as she paddled the seaplane closer. He felt the passion rising, not for sex, but to have her at his command, to sketch and work with brush and oils until he had captured her cool exterior, the hidden fire burning underneath.

Later, he had watched her take off, entranced by the beauty of wing-tips flying overhead, the knowledge that the beautiful bird was controlled by a restrained mystery woman. What did he know about her? Eyes that held heat and depth, an enigma concealing herself from the world. To paint her he would have to know something of what lay hidden below.

He had noticed when the engine shifted tone, but attached no significance. Aeroplanes were always doing that, engine sounds changing, alarming passengers who thought it meant something.

Then, out of sight, the noise stopped entirely, the echo of her engine haunting him. His heart stopped too, started again a split second later when the sound resumed. For just a moment he had thought... he had felt panic, his heart thundering as if it were *his* life about to end.

She had returned, searching under the engine cover, then anchoring the plane. When he came close, he found her eyes uneasy. Why was she frightened of him? She was a woman who had confidence, walked equally with men, yet on the pontoon of the Cessna she had tried to scurry past him quickly, had slipped and trembled when he pulled her tight against him to save her from the cold waters.

She had been firm and soft and woman in his arms. He had never felt anything quite so good as her slender body twisting in his arms. It was not a painting he wanted then. He wanted *her*, this woman, writhing and moaning in his arms. More than anything, he wanted her to want him, to feel as he did, this crazy, insane, totally overwhelming passion.

Where the hell was the father of that kid? What was the score? Why was she living on an expensive yacht, yet flying as a bush pilot, looking like an angel with that cloud of fair hair?

He called to her, 'OK, dinner's ready!' She did not answer. At first he had intended to deliver her dinner into the salon. After all, she must be tired. Those charter companies flew all the long daylight hours, and this time of year dawn was around five, and sunset about ten at night.

He admitted to himself that he had called out to her because he wanted to see the curve of her hip through his soft jogging pants as she climbed the two steps up to the wheelhouse. He needed to watch the swing of her hair as she moved. Pretty crazy, because that elusive memory told him that the lady was trouble.

Why? Where had he seen her before?

He loaded the soup and sandwiches on to the tray, poured a glass of reconstituted frozen orange juice into a glass. A spoon. A piece of paper towel to substitute for a napkin. That would have to do. He carried the tray in one hand, switching on the light on the salon ceiling as he went down the stairs, ducking his head from habit as he stepped into the salon with its lower ceiling, stopping abruptly when he saw her.

She was asleep, curled up precariously on the narrow settee near the stove, her face in shadow. She was huddled under her jacket as if it were not enough, her legs drawn up to warm her torso and her arm curled around the legs. Why hadn't she asked for a blanket?

He put the tray down and cleared some canvases off the wide settee on the far side of the cabin. He didn't have an extra sheet, but there was a soft quilt that would feel good to sleep on. It was massively wide, and he knew from his own experience that it felt very good to curl up in. He spread it out on the big settee and arranged the extra to draw over her.

When he crossed the cabin and bent to slip his arms under her, she came as if she belonged there, her face turning into his shoulder, her hand spreading against his chest.

He sat down on the big settee with her in his arms, feeling her warmth against his lap, his chest. He knew he should slide her out of his arms and on to the blanket, but she was nestling against, him, twisting slightly in her sleep, as if her sleeping body knew his and was at home in his arms. Her face was still and very vulnerable, very young, her lips parted slightly. He bent his head and felt the faint breath from her lungs, her warmth against his face. Her lashes were darker than her hair, full and soft against her cheeks. She wore no make-up at all. No mascara. No lipstick.

He could feel her woman's curves through the softness of the jogging pants she wore. He looked down at the pressure of her full breasts against the thin blouse she wore. It was the first time he had ever seen her without a jacket. Her breasts were surprisingly full for such a long, leggy blonde. Nice, just barely this side of voluptuous.

He wished he had stripped his shirt off as he worked in the kitchen. It was a strong fantasy vision, but if he had, her hand would be tangled in the hair of his chest, her breath warm against his skin.

It was the powerful urge to touch where his eyes rested that actually brought him to his senses. He could not fondle a sleeping woman, for heaven's sake! What did he think he was doing? Fighting with her while she was awake, stroking while she slept? It would be the worst sort of invasion of privacy.

He turned and leaned, sliding her body on to the settee behind him. As if she felt nervous of falling, her arms reached up and clung to his shoulders. He found himself holding her close with both arms returning her embrace, feeling all that wonderful softness clinging to him, his heart pounding and his body fully aroused.

'Angel, I've got to let go of you,' he whispered, leaning down with her to ease her shoulders on to the mattress. How could she be the woman his half-memory thought, yet feel like this in his arms?

He moved back, slipping away, but she was still clinging. 'Where were you?' Her voice was husky, sleepy, her eyes still closed. Her arms were a warm prison and her lips seemed to be parting just for him.

'In the galley.' His voice was choked, his arteries pounding, pulsing wild from a heart that should know to keep still. He should get his arms away from her, get that blanket over her, run as far and as fast as he could.

She twisted, thrusting her leg out, turning towards him, one arm still holding his shoulders and the other reaching up to caress his neck. Her hair was streaming all around her. He found his fingers moving to it, stroking and caressing, loving the glorious, shiny stuff.

Was she sleeping? Awake? He didn't know, but this was unfair advantage. He must not——

Her lips parted farther. She moaned slightly, the sound destroying anything resembling rational thought in his mind. He watched the tip of her pink tongue caressing her upper lip in a sensual motion. He must touch his lips to hers, just once, before he could let her go.

He bent over her. She tasted of honey, sweet and wild, her lips moving under his. 'I was waiting,' she whispered against his lips. 'Where were you? I waited so long.'

CHAPTER FOUR

It was another of those endless nights.

Waiting, half sleeping, listening for Tyler to come home. Would he ever be here, beside her? Would it ever again be as it had in those first days, before their marriage?

How many nights? How many hours, lying alone, wanting to be touched, to be loved? She was aching inside, yet freezing from the outside in, the loneliness growing and imprisoning her heart. She could not seem to keep herself from hoping, from believing that this was only temporary. He would come back once the new client was dealt with, the campaign won.

She would not let herself cry, but she listened, a hard tension growing over the aching. *Tyler, I love you.* It was starting to hurt when she said the words to herself, and she never said them to Tyler any more. He never wanted to hear.

She drifted on a cloud of weariness, half dreaming, half sleeping. In the moments when sleep and dreams mingled, she must have missed the sound of the door, of Tyler's footsteps on the stairs. Usually she woke instantly, listening, hoping he would come here, wanting to be with her. Usually he went into the next room, sleeping alone on the single bed rather than disturbing her. More and more often, he did not come at all, claiming that it was simpler to sleep on the couch in his office.

Tonight he had slipped in while she slept. At first the touch of his hands was part of the dream, the fantasy.

Then she was held securely in his arms, feeling the thundering of his heart, her hand spread out against the hardness of his chest.

It had been so long. He must have been working out in the gym to get this new hardness. She curled against him, knowing that if she opened her eyes he would be gone, the image dissolved.

The longing was pounding in her veins, heating her everywhere, leaving her trembling. She turned in his arms, feeling the closeness she had needed so long, clinging desperately when he lowered her to the soft bed, terrified he would leave her alone again.

He was her husband, but she was terribly afraid of losing him. 'Where were you?' she whispered, but his answer made no sense, his voice odd in the night. The galley?

Don't go! she cried without words. She touched him, wanting, then his hands were in her hair, caressing with a new softness that brought a low moan from her throat. Her lips parted, her fingers curving into the flesh of his neck.

When his lips took hers, it was as if her heart filled, overflowed, shuddering waves of need and loneliness filling from his touch, warmth and tongues touching with slow passion.

She couldn't stop the words, the need and aching inside. It seemed to fill her, to flow over. 'I was waiting,' she confessed, her body pressing against his, her curves into his hardness, her woman unable to hold back the need for this man. She knew she must not ask questions, but could not keep back, 'Where were you? I waited so long.'

The touch on her lips was fleeting, a strange tickling against her cheek. She turned her face to him, felt her hair pulling as his fingers threaded through the softness.

She groaned as the light touch of his hands grazed the curve of her breast, the thrust of her hips.

Wildness, heat, pulsing. He had hardly touched, so soft and careful, but her heart was responding, moistening her body, swelling the thrust of her breasts, bringing her to a peak of need she had never felt before. Such a long, barren time of loneliness.

She reached, threading her fingers through soft hair, pulling herself close against a muscular chest. Her lips parted, inviting his kiss, her eyelids half open, eyes unfocused.

Tongue plundering her mouth, taking as if she belonged, as if no other touch would satisfy. Soft bristling against her cheek, her chin. She rolled her head, confused, inflamed by the gentle firmness of hands along her back, a hard palm taking possession of her buttocks, holding her against a man's implacable need.

Her groan was formless, her woman's warmth opening, her hip thrusting as one leg curled over his, feeling the roughness of denim.

But Tyler never wore jeans.

Her mouth. His lips teasing hers, biting without teeth, a tongue exploring the warm darkness inside. She was spinning, sensations and touches confusing and inflaming. She lost control of her neck, the firmness eroding under exploring fingers, moist tongue.

When her head fell back on the pillow, his mouth followed the curve of her neck, the soft bristles an erotic tickling; the moist, gentle tongue and lips sending flames everywhere along the softness of her trembling throat, down the V of her shirt and against the soft flesh that would lead to her breasts.

Fingers against her breast, heated through the thin cotton. She felt the blouse parting, her chest swelling, trying to burst from the restraint of a lacy bra.

The bra. Why was she wearing it while she slept? Why were his fingers such a delicious roughness against her skin? And that soft bristling against her, the sensuous roughness as his lips touched, his...

She gasped as her nipple was drawn into warm moistness, her hands clutching the hardness of broad shoulders, fingers fumbling to find the flesh under the fabric of his shirt. Somewhere she knew it was wrong, something was wrong, but she could not think, could feel only the pulsing need, the frantic ecstasy of touching and caressing the breadth of his hard shoulders, the length of hair, the trembling rigidity of a chest finally freed of clothes.

'Is this what you like, angel?'

The words hardly penetrated the thunder in her ears. He had never touched her like this before, the soft tongue stroking, inflaming, moving from one bursting breast to the other, sending her spinning into a dark, sensuous nowhere where her head rolled against the pillow.

Was it his hands? She could not seem to separate the feelings. Touches, kisses. Fingers exploring gently, stroking her trembling midriff, her swollen breasts. When he kissed the soft skin of her midriff, she thought she would go mad with the wanting, then somehow his mouth was exploring the curve of her belly and she was only a mass of shuddering need, her hands frantic on him, worrying at the barriers between them, the denim and the soft flannel.

Then there was no barrier. She thought he must have swept away the clothes with a magic touch. There was only her trembling, naked softness pressed against the long, hard length of him. Her fingers tangled in the hair of his chest, his hands holding her close, touching where his lips touched.

There was a moment when he moved away, when she reached out in panic and a low voice growled, 'It's all right, angel. I just want to look at you.'

Cool air against her naked flesh. She opened her eyes, her breathing ragged. Everything was strange, impossible like a dream. He was only inches away, propped up on an elbow, looking down along the length of her. There was a light behind him, emphasising the wildness of dark hair and full beard.

A dream. It had to be a dream, all of it. This man naked beside her, his eyes taking her as if it were his right, as if she were a woman who belonged to him. She had not had a forced landing, was not stranded in the middle of nowhere with a wild man who had touched and kissed her as if——

Her legs were parted for him, her nipples hard peaks of desire on passion-swollen mounds. There was nothing to cover her. Something in his eyes penetrated too deeply for her to withdraw from him. It was as if she were held here, a prisoner of something that had grown in her sleep.

'What is your name?' Was that her voice, husky and passionate? She must cover the places his eyes moved, somehow push down everything inside her, the feelings that had burst out of nowhere as if they would never be imprisoned again.

'Matthew,' he said, his hand lying on his naked hip. She saw his lips curve slightly as he spoke, then his arm moved and she could do nothing but watch as his fingers came close to her, caressed the peak of one breast, gently rolling her hardened arousal between finger and thumb.

'Beautiful,' he whispered, bending to place his lips where fingers had been, to suck gently, sending the intimate kiss through her whole being, leaving her a helpless shuddering in front of his devouring gaze.

'No,' she whispered, the panic only half heard in her voice. 'Don't!' He drew back and she was choked, could say no more, could only stare into the darkness that was his eyes, shadowed from the light by his own body.

Then he reached back, up, stretching the muscles across his chest, his abdomen hardening as he stretched his arm. His hand grasped. There was a click. Then darkness, the light gone, nothing outside but the wild darkness, water and sleeping trees.

'No, angel, you don't want me to stop.' The low voice was a growl. She could not see, but stared at his face, knowing his lips were parted, an invitation for her kiss; as if she would flow up against him and take his tongue into the darkness of her mouth, take his manhood into her warm, moist woman.

She was shivering, trembling. When his fingers trailed along the softness of her breast, down along the firm curves of her waist, her hips, she could not stop the sharp intake of air through her teeth, the tongue that wet her dry lips.

He leaned to her, took her lips with his as her tongue disappeared. 'Don't ask me to stop,' he groaned against her, his mouth leaving a trail of molten desire across her cheek, down the tender vulnerability of her throat.

She had pressed her legs tightly together, but his fingers stroked where the flesh of her inner thigh was pressed tight. Inside her there started a trembling she could not stop.

'No,' she whispered, but his lips were taking everything, his hands caressing the fullness of her breasts as he bent down, kissed the trembling of her abdomen, the wild pulsing of her thighs.

'You're everything,' he groaned against her soft, wild warmth. 'Beautiful...soft...hot.' He touched her, made her groan with need, and there was no denial left in her, only the wonderful closeness of feeling, touching, closeness.

Her lips sought the fluttering vulnerability of his eyes, kissing his lids closed. Her hands touched, exploring the hard rigidity of his chest, driven on by the latent wild desires he was rousing, the forgotten woman inside surging to a wild, passionate life that went far beyond anything she had experienced before. Between the gasps he drew from her, with his lips and hands and the hardness of his body, she explored the rigid cords of muscles, the line of a scar that she could not see.

He shifted and she was lying half on top of him, his lips murmuring. 'That's better. I've got both hands free for you.' She gloried in the journeys his roaming fingers pursued. She touched, too, finding the soft places on him, then touching so that his head arched back and he groaned loudly, 'Ooohh—I need you, angel!'

His body was trembling hard against her. 'I need to be inside you, loving you.' His hands were everywhere, her own hands clutching him, burying in the curling hairs of his chest as his lips returned to take her mouth again.

It was in her, too, the surging pulse, the shuddering ache that must be satisfied. She did not hear the words she whispered, the shuddering need deep in her own eyes. She dreamed that she could see his eyes, half covered by drooping lids as his hard hands trembled against her, became suddenly firm and sure as he guided her over him.

Her heart stopped when he lowered her, his hands on her hips, his own body thrusting from below. He filled her and she needed more, movement and the hard growth of his desire. There was a wild ascent, a frantic rhythm, words whispered and groaned . . . then the spinning, pulsing fulfilment that left her only a weak, trembling collection of collapsed muscles and tremblingly satisfied passion.

She fell against his broad chest, shuddering, weak with the passage of all the emotions. Somewhere there was a part of her that knew morning would come, and regret; but his arms came around her and she could feel only his trembling, his soft words saying, 'Sleep, angel. Lie here in my arms and sleep,' his breath against her cheek as she obeyed.

Smooth darkness, warm and secure. In moments of half-wakefulness she twisted, felt the pressure of a hard male leg thrown over hers, strong arms holding her. Once she almost woke, but a low murmuring sent her back to sleep. She could not remember the words, but the darkness came again and she knew no more.

The faint lightening of the pre-dawn sky finally woke her, the blackness outside turning to black and grey, then colours coming as the sun rose.

Time to be in the air, flying.

She felt the familiar motion under her, the boat riding on a slight movement of water. She pushed back on her hair, found a wild, unfamiliar tangle catching at her fingers. What had she been doing? Thrashing in her sleep, sending hair into a tangled knot that——

Strange memories flushed her cheek, then her movement brought her up against a hard warmth and her eyes flew open, reality flooding in.

Mountain Man, lying beside her, his arm thrown out, curving up against the wall at the other side of the bunk, the new dawn showing him to her. His chest was bare, two red lines drawn on the hard bulge of his male breast.

Her fingernails. His thrust sending her wild, her hands and fingers digging into the hardness of his chest as his hands held her, guided her against his passionate need.

Oh, God!

This had to be a dream, some insane fantasy. Him. Lying beside her, his body sprawled, leg thrown out against her. He looked...

Matthew. The name had been whispered somewhere in the midst of the wild, erotic dream. She shivered, wondering if it had really seemed a dream, or if the heat rising in her had enticed her to push away reality, not willing to open her eyes until she was...satisfied.

No man had ever made love to her like that. There had never been anyone but Tyler, the man she should not have loved, and he had never touched her like that, kissed her in places that destroyed everything but needing and passion and a warm, hot, womanly something that had welled up and taken possession of her.

Matthew.

The sun would climb over the horizon, and he would wake. He would look at her and——

Would he want her again? Lying beside him, looking at the way the quilt half exposed the hard bareness of his chest, she could feel desire stirring inside, her eyes following the lines and ridges of him.

He was long and lean, but now, without clothing to conceal, she could see all the hard muscles she had only guessed at before. She wanted to reach out and touch, stroke the curling dark hairs high on his chest, follow the swirling pattern to where it disappeared under the casual fold of the quilt.

If she did, he would wake. He would turn and it would be in his eyes, all the things that had been in his voice in the night. Desire and——

His arm moved, seeking her, and she stumbled out from the covers, bolting, panicked. If he touched her—oh, God! If he touched her, she thought she would turn into the woman from last night again. Mindless needing and wanting. It was—this was not her, not the Nicole Bentham who was Shane's mother.

If she had been hurt by Tyler, what would this man do? At least there had been something predictable about Tyler. Mountain Man—Matthew——

It was only sex. He had wanted her, and taken her, and she was the one trembling and shaken down to the places that had always stayed firm and untouched.

She had to get out of here, away, far from him, had to stop standing here and staring at him, stop that wanton part of her that wondered what would happen if she reached out and pulled aside the quilt, or if she went back, lay down beside him, moving against him.

Madness, a woman of her age acting like a wanton child with no responsibilities! She looked around desperately, found the soft greyness of his jogging pants.

He had removed her clothes.

She jerked them on, stumbling in the long softness before she got the elastic ankles pulled up. Where were her jeans? Her shirt? She froze as his low voice caressed her.

'Morning, angel.'

She did not want to look down at him. He should cover up, conceal the tangles of hair on his chest. Oh, damn! She couldn't seem to get hold, to stop herself from looking at the raggedness of his beard, remembering how it had felt against her, how his hands and his lips had created ecstasy, taking her on the journey they had shared.

She jerked back a step, the back of her thighs coming hard into the edge of a table. She licked her lips, wished she could look away.

'Come here, angel.' His arm spread out, inviting. His voice was husky with sleep. 'Come and say good morning.'

'No!' It was choked out, a ragged protest that sounded like nothing.

His eyebrows lifted slightly, his beard covering any expression except for the narrowing of his eyes. He sat up, the quilt falling away. She retreated a step along the edge of the table, towards the steps that led up to the wheelhouse.

'Don't——' Her protest echoed, unfinished.

'Don't what?' His voice was the one she remembered from before, cool and frosty. Then his eyes fell from her face to the exposed roundness of her breasts, and she saw that he still wanted her.

She covered herself, crossing her arms over her chest too late to conceal the tightening of her nipples, the visible betrayal of her own reaction.

She whispered, 'Please, don't—I don't want to...'

He stood up, leaving the covers behind, coming too close to her but not touching, and he was wearing nothing. She did not want to look. She remembered his body too well, with a painful, passionate clarity swathed in dreams.

He echoed softly, 'You don't want to?' He touched the swelling where her folded arms had pushed up her breasts. He held her eyes as his fingers brushed the tops of her breasts, and he could see when her pupils dilated.

He was dangerous, too damned attractive and too desirable. When she looked in his eyes and saw the way he wanted her, she had to grit her teeth to stop her arms from reaching out, touching him, offering everything.

She was Nicole, the ice lady, all coolness and control. And he had touched her; now all she wanted was to let his touch find the trembling places again.

'You——' She was shaking. It had to stop. She pulled back, a little more in control when his fingers fell away. How could he touch her like that, as if she were his for taking? As if she belonged to anyone who wanted? She had to fight him, somehow cover what was trembling all through her.

'You,' he whispered, then he was closer. She could feel the rising heat from his flesh. 'You want me as much as I want you, angel.'

For an instant she was lost, moving to him, then his words found some chord in her mind and the anger came. She grabbed desperately at the emotion, as foreign to her as passion. The blazing heat grew inside, turning everything she could see to red, bathing her in a protective covering, safe from the trembling need.

She had never shouted at anyone else, only him. Screaming scenes made her sick, threw her into a silent panic. Yet now her voice was rising, flaring, out of control, all the fury from nowhere hurled at him.

'You think this is such a damned casual thing? That you can seduce women in their sleep? Who the hell do you think you are?'

The softness left him, and the desire with it. His jaw clenched with anger and he moved closer, deliberately towering over her. There was a terrible silent moment, then she got a ragged breath into her lungs and said, 'Macho, aren't you? Do you get a kick out of this? Standing all muscles and threats over a woman? Taking advantage?'

He exploded. 'Listen, angel! I wasn't the one that did the seducing. It was you! You were the one that fastened your arms around my neck and wouldn't let go. You cuddled your soft body against me and——'

She gasped, ears spinning, the dizzy throbbing in her veins surging up. 'Stop it!' She covered flaming cheeks with her hands, trying to push the memories away. What had been the dream? What the reality? Had it all been his hands, his arms? Her wildness?

They were both silent, breathing heavily as if from a race, staring at each other with anger. She spoke first, breathlessly yet angrily. 'You're a selfish bastard, taking advantage. I was asleep, not—did it ever occur to you that you might get me pregnant?'

'No. Not for an instant.' She bit her lip and he said stonily, 'Don't be ridiculous. You're a married woman. If you weren't on some kind of birth control, you'd have more than one child by now.'

She swallowed, hurt half-exposed in her eyes. He knew nothing about her. He did not know who she was, what she was; yet he thought she was married, casually turning into another's arms for a night of pleasure.

She said tightly, feeling a familiar coolness that meant control. 'That's your thing, is it? Married women? Doesn't it bother you to seduce a—to take a woman who belongs to another man? If you thought I——'

He snorted in exasperation. 'Angel, I didn't do a hell of a lot of thinking. I haven't had a woman in weeks, and you were there, and you were willing, even eager.'

'I was not! I was sleeping! And I haven't——'

Her voice rang around them. There had never been anyone but the man she married, and that was all so long ago, it was a wonder she could remember that she was a woman. He was staring at her, waiting until he said very quietly, 'You haven't what?'

She shook her head and there was something in her face, a wild distress that he recognised. Remembered.

'It was in a newspaper,' he said slowly, and he saw her face go grey and ashen. 'Not just one newspaper. All of them, your face everywhere.'

She looked like a frozen thing. He closed his eyes, trying to bring back half-remembered mental pictures, the white panic of her face distracting him. He had a memory that was virtually photographic for things he had read, pictures he had seen. Where had he been? When?

'Vancouver,' he said. 'It was in Vancouver. It was in the local papers.'

'Please don't,' she whispered. 'Matthew, please don't.' He did not seem to hear a word she said. He was going to remember, bring it all back, the pain and the loss and the loneliness.

He closed his eyes and she suddenly saw her shirt lying in a tumbled heap at the bottom of the bunk. She reached for it, pulled it on and fumbled with the buttons. She had no idea where her bra was, but right now she did not care. She had to cover herself, get away.

She never went without a bra, did not care to have the free fullness of her breasts attracting speculative looks from men she did not want. She did not want any man to come close. There had been enough hurt to last her for ever. If she could get away from here, away from him, she might manage to forget last night had ever happened.

'Four years ago.' This was a puzzle to him, and slowly he was going to remember. She could see it in his face, his eyes. Damn the man!

Her jacket was lying on the table. Her shoes—there! Near the stove. She pulled them on as he said, 'You said your name was Nick, but that's not a woman's name. It wasn't Nick, was it?'

'Nicole,' she said unwillingly, her shoes on, the laces almost done. It would take him time to get dressed. If she made a break for it in his dinghy, she did not think he would chase her like that, naked.

'Nicole,' he agreed. His eyes were watching, but did not seem to really see what she was doing. She supposed that was the artist in him, the man who thought in pictures, looking harder at past pictures than the one in front of him as he said, 'There was an accident.'

Her husband, and yet another woman...Tyler...dead.

He was frowning, not quite getting the memory clear. 'It was a real mess,' he said slowly, watching her now, seeing every detail, his eyes growing hard. Her tumbled blonde hair, the parted lips. He said harshly, 'Last night you could almost have convinced me that you were a woman starved for love.' She shivered at his memories, slowly backed up the stairs. She was standing above him, looking down, and there was nothing but scorn in his eyes.

'Matthew——'

'I didn't read all the details, but I remember enough.' He laughed, a painfully harsh sound breaking through the red dawn. 'That's hilarious! Outraged innocence! A minute ago you almost had me believing it, that you were a faithful wife, that last night was—but this is nothing new for you, is it? You're used to taking your pleasure where you find it. Is this act your usual procedure? Is this how you justified yourself when your husband was alive? Outraged innocence? That's a hell of a laugh.'

'No!' She closed her eyes painfully, bewildered and confused by this line of attack. 'What are you talking about? I've never—this is the first time I've ever—ever——'

He snorted, his eyes filled with scorn and...hatred. 'Don't try to fool me, lady. You weren't exactly the innocent four years ago! Where were you while your husband was off having a wild weekend with that actress? As I recall, you were off in the north somewhere, having your own affair with a man twice your age.'

She gasped. 'Oh, God, Matthew! No! I—I——' She shook her head, the tears welling up. He moved a step toward her and she turned in panic, fleeing along the length of the wheelhouse before he could see the tears.

'How wrong can I have it?' He was right behind her, his fingers brushing, almost catching her, not letting her escape. She flung the door open and burst into the cockpit, looking wildly for the dinghy. Thank goodness he had not brought it aboard last night, but had left it floating in the water beside them.

She climbed on to the deck, one step ahead of him, trying not to listen as he said coldly, 'You proved the case last night, didn't you? You've certainly learned how to please a man.' His voice was suddenly raw, accusing, and she gasped, choking, hurting because somehow he had to know that was exactly what she had not been able to do. Please a man. Hold a man. He said tightly, 'Quite a bit of experience.'

There was the dinghy line. She bent to untie it, had it in her hand before he realised what she was doing. He was standing in the cockpit, glaring up at her on the deck, and he started to shout, 'Hey, what the hell do you think you're doing?'

She did not waste breath or time on an answer. She pulled the dinghy towards her, stepped over and jumped, hoping that it would work and she would not end up in the water, wet and cold and stranded while he watched, or laughed.

She pushed hard on the side of the boat, floating away just as his hand shot down, grasping desperately for her, for the dinghy, for anything.

'Hey——'

'I'm leaving,' she said when she was beyond his reach. She gulped a couple of deep breaths, staring back at him as he stood on the deck of his boat. He still had no clothes on, as if chasing after her were more important than modesty.

She slapped hard at the voice inside that told her to go back to him. She groped desperately for the coldness, the ice that was fear inside her. When she had it, she held his eyes as hard as she could with her own. 'I hope you were satisfied with our...our little *interlude*.' She swallowed, feeling the trembling starting inside, and said, 'Personally, I've had better.'

Then she got away, paddling and not looking back, hoping the electrical tape would be enough to repair the wiring problem and that the magneto would let her take off quickly, before he found a way to stop her.

CHAPTER FIVE

SHE heard his engine starting as she got the cowling off the top of the Cessna's engine, and she almost dropped the roll of electrical tape into the water at the sound.

That was all she needed, to have the tape floating in the water—would it float, or sink? She would have to chase after it, or beg some from Matthew.

Her fingers trembled as she checked the wire. It was all right except for the damaged insulation at the fire wall. She gently pulled it to gain access to the damaged part, carefully twisted five or six turns of the black plastic tape over it, then pulled and broke off the tape, smoothing the edge back on to the wire.

With the wire pushed back into the fire wall, the repair was complete. With any luck she would be in the air before Luke turned up with the replacement magneto that she did not need.

Before Mountain Man got over here with his boat. He was doing something. What? He was out on deck. Yes, of course. He would be pulling up anchor. That would delay him, thank goodness!

How deep was the water here where she had anchored the seaplane? She had intended to free his dinghy, leave it floating for him to pick up, but if the water was too shallow for *Charmaine*'s keel, he would have no choice but to swim for the dinghy.

She did not want to torture him by forcing him into that cold northern water. People had been known to die of exposure within ten or twenty minutes, and she did not want him suffering from hypothermia out here all alone.

She simply wanted to get away, never to see him again.

She left the dinghy tied to the float while she untied the jerry cans from the wings and put them into the luggage compartment. Then she pulled up her own anchor. When she felt the resistance of the mud bottom, she crouched down on the pontoon and pulled hard, then measured the depth with her arms as she pulled in the last of the rope.

It was borderline. Perhaps eight or nine feet of water under her. *Charmaine* probably had a draft of about six feet. If the bottom was irregular he might go aground trying to retrieve the dinghy.

All right. She would paddle the plane into the middle of the bay, towing the dinghy. Then she would set it free.

It all took so damned long, and he had the anchor up long before she was clear of the shallows. One minute he was on the other side of the cove, then she heard the engine and looked up, and found him only fifty feet away.

She stopped and he eased closer, then he must have put the sail-boat into neutral because he was drifting closer, stepping out on to the deck, dressed in jeans and nothing else, bare feet and chest.

She stopped paddling. She did not want to get much closer. From here she could not see his eyes, and he could not see whatever might be in her face.

'Just let the dinghy free!' His voice echoed off the trees. 'I'll pick it up from there!'

She nodded, keeping her head down while she fitted the paddle into its holder on the pontoon, untied the painter and pushed the dinghy towards the hull of the boat.

When she stood up and grasped the door to open it, his boat was much closer. He had made no move to manoeuvre it into position to pick up the dinghy, but was watching her, his face rather frighteningly solemn. His engine was quiet. Had he turned it off? They were close enough to talk in the silence, but she did not know what to say to him, although it seemed there should be something.

She stood up and grasped the door to the cockpit.

'Angel?'

Why did he have to call her that? It was a name that belonged with the night, the dreaming and the passion. She climbed into her seat.

'Be careful on the flight home.' He sounded as if it mattered to him. She flipped a switch on the console, the door still open.

Without looking, she called back to him, 'I'm always careful.'

Once she had the engine started there could be no talk. She would not hear, and that would be a good thing. She would be gone, wings against the sky.

'I believe that.' His voice was low, crossing the water, penetrating the link between her mind and her hands. 'But, angel, you don't usually fly when you're this upset.'

Matthew had upset her. His fault. When she had this bird in the air, the soaring flight would free her of these feelings. Flying would dissolve this inexplicable urge to turn to a man who seemed to desire her and despise her at one and the same time.

'I'm sorry I frightened you, angel.'

The air left her lungs, disappeared in an instant, and she was breathless. She stared at him through the windscreen, could not seem to break her eyes free. She had a terrible feeling that he could see through her to everything.

Right now, with that look in his eyes, if she stepped out and got the plane to him, climbed back up on to his boat, she could tell him everything.

He would understand once she explained, and they would go back inside. Then——

She forced a lump that could not be tears past the place in her throat that was an impossible barrier. She could not be feeling like this! As if she could walk into his arms and dissolve into him, lose her identity.

He wanted her. Want. Desire. Sex. There was no love, just the physical. But inside her was an awful trembling softness. It would only take a touch, a look, and she would be a trembling thing at his feet, begging him for...love.

As she had begged Tyler for his love. No! She would not succumb to that cruel fate again, loving, caring, needing so much more than the man who said he wanted her.

She did not love him! You could not love a man after only a few hours' total contact! Add it up, Nicole! Counting the confrontation over Shane, what was it? How many hours? Did you count the sleeping time? Two bodies tangled together as one?

It was impossible to pull her eyes away from his, but her hands moved and the engine fired, and she moved the seaplane along the water. That was the only way she could break that long, painful contact, his eyes taking possession of her, silently.

He was not a man who talked a lot. This morning, arguing with her, responding to her accusations and throwing his own, he had spoken more than in all the days his boat was tied beside hers. And last night, in the real dream of his arms and his kisses, he had told her she was a beautiful creature, an angel, a woman for his man.

The rest of the time he was mostly silent, yet she always felt she knew his thoughts, as if the conversation were running while the silence filled.

'Be careful.'

She would not look back, but his voice was in her ears, reminding her to do all the things that made the difference between the old pilots and the bold pilots.

She must have been almost a baby the first time she heard her father talk about the bold pilots. She always flew with him, belted into the co-pilot's seat of his little Cessna, listening to him go through his pre-flight check, telling her each step.

'Don't ever forget to check the mags before you take off,' he had told her as they gained speed. 'Once you've got her revved up, you can check. First the left, then the right. Wait until she's up on the step if you want, just about to take off, but be sure you do it before you're in the air. Remember, Nikki. There are old pilots, and there are bold pilots; but there are no old, bold pilots.'

The wind was right for a take-off down the channel away from *Charmaine*, and it was easier when he was behind her, out of sight, although his voice was still in her ears, mingled with her father's.

The mags checked OK, thank goodness!

It was not her best take-off, but she was airborne and the habits had taken over, her hands and the part of her mind that had been flying since she was a child doing all the right things, sealing off the quivering panic that had threatened to smother her back there on the ground.

She got Barry on the radio just as she glanced down and saw *Charmaine*'s tiny foreshortened mast passing below her. 'Tell Luke it's OK. A shorted wire. I taped it and I'm on my way in.'

'Luke's just loading up,' he told her. 'You'll probably be on the ground before he takes off for the west coast.

Shane's going with him. It's a big rigmarole. It's going to be several flights, take most of the day.'

When she landed, Shane caught her wing and manoeuvred the Cessna against the dock, then started securing the pontoons. Luke climbed up on to the co-pilot's seat.

'You got it fixed?'

She nodded. 'Insulating shield was gone at the fire wall. I put tape on it this morning when I could see well enough.'

He nodded approval. 'I'm glad you didn't try to fly her back with one mag. We'll replace that wire before she goes up. Are you all right?' The question came swiftly, unexpectedly, and she found her face flaming.

'What—what do you mean?'

'That's not the way you were dressed when you left. What happened?'

'Oh. The pants.' She stared at the grey fabric covering her legs. Her jeans were back at Matthew's boat. Her panties and bra, too, although their absence was concealed from Luke's disturbed gaze. 'I—it's nothing. I slipped on the pontoon and got wet.'

Matthew. He had been holding her tightly, her breasts and her abdomen, her thighs pressed closely against him. Nicole gulped, said, 'I had to beg some dry clothes.'

Luke was frowning, worried by something in her voice or her face. 'Nick, you—he didn't try anything, did he?' She shook her head and he said, disturbed, 'Look, I—you're so damned good at looking after yourself. When I sent you out on these flights, I never thought there might be some danger that——'

'No!' She gulped, looked away from him, saw her son outside working.

Damn Luke! Why did he have to be so quietly observant? He cared about her, heaven knew why. There was no sex in it. He adored his wife, couldn't keep his eyes off the vivacious, dark-haired Laurie whenever she was anywhere near. He simply was a nice man who cared about other people. Her father had been a nice man, too, but she had not known many others.

She swallowed, managed something that might have been a smile if she had not been trembling. 'Luke, I—if anything happened, it—I—nothing happened that I didn't . . . didn't want.'

She turned away then and clambered out of the Cessna. In the days that followed, part of her wanted to run away from the memory of Matthew, run far and fast. Another part wanted to set sail, go out to the west coast and find him again.

If she did, a voice whispered that this time it would be slower. There were misunderstandings to heal, and they needed to get to know each other. It would be so easy to walk back into his arms, into his bed, but there was so much more in his eyes. Deep inside, a voice told her that this man could give her all the things that she had never had, that he was the man Tyler had never been, the man of her dreams. How could she walk away from the kind of feelings he had been able to stir inside her?

Those thoughts belonged to the nights and the sky, the lonely hours after Shane was asleep, and the soaring freedom of flight high above the hills.

When she had her feet on land, and the sun shining through the illusions, she remembered that he was a wild man, a wanderer without roots; that she was a woman who had already made one very bad mistake in choosing a mate. She was not really crazy enough to go searching for a man like him, but she wished she could stop dreaming about him.

He had not even tried, and she had been melting in his arms. She had been willing, eager, pressing against him in her half-sleep, wanting and inviting. All right. Fair enough. But she *had* been asleep. What kind of a man took advantage of that? To hell with the male of the species and his damned desires, his male sex drive. What did she want with a man who would not even stop, wait for a time when she was awake and . . . and willing? If it was that easy for him to take her, to bend his head and take her lips, brushing her cheek with the soft roughness of his beard . . . If——

Oh, damn! Why did her mind keep returning to that, to his touch, his closeness? Why did it rouse such a hunger in her? Not just desire, the sensual need, but also a deep soul-hunger for this man close again.

She did not *want* to feel like this, yet sometimes, when she woke in the morning she would throw on her robe and dash out into the cockpit, half expecting, hoping that *Charmaine* would be there, tied against her boat.

In the last few years only this one man had touched her, and all her declarations and convictions that she wanted only to be alone were destroyed . . . almost destroyed.

She would never see him again. The days were going, the memories—she hoped—starting to fade. God! How long could one night retain such a hold on her mind? Surely not much longer? In less than a week, she and Shane would be leaving for their two-week sailing holiday before the school year began. They would go to the east coast of the islands, not the west. She would never, *never* see Matthew again.

If she could have buried herself in Shane's company, doing things with him, it might have been possible to escape the paths her mind kept taking. But Shane had taken to his work at QC Air with unprecedented enthusiasm. He had found a hero in Luke, seemed happy to do any menial job that would put him near the aeroplanes.

If she thought that the new passion with flying would supplant Shane's long-standing preoccupation with drawing, she was wrong. He began to take his sketch-pad with him on the flights he shared with Luke.

If it weren't for that night they had shared, she might have gone looking for Matthew, to ask his advice about Shane's talent. She had a feeling that he was very successful, and that his ideas might be invaluable to Shane. The day after she saw Matthew's paintings off in their taxi to the airport, Barry had received a phone call from an almost hysterical Lyndon Boydon. He had handed the receiver to her.

'Those paintings have got to be here by Friday! They simply must! Matt has to take this seriously! This is a big show, and if the canvases aren't there——'

'Mr Boydon, I'm sure they'll be there. The taxi took them out to Sandspit Airport yesterday morning. They'll be air express on today's plane. They'll probably be delivered to you this afternoon.'

He had calmed down then, said, 'Thanks, Miss—what's your name?'

'Nicole. Nicole Bentham.' She had smiled a little. This man was almost like a child, frantic one minute, grateful the next.

'The lad who answered the phone said you were the pilot who flew out for the paintings.'

'That's right.'

'Nothing got damaged, did it? I shudder when I think of Matt tossing invaluable works of art in and out of seaplanes.' His voice became higher-pitched as he described his mental agonies.

'Nothing was damaged. He was very careful, and so was I.' She was grinning now, wondering how Matthew handled this man. Barry was watching, listening to her side of the conversation, openly curious.

'How is the boy?' The voice on the telephone lowered, said confidentially, 'He's a genius, you know. But I worry about him. He's always off somewhere, at the end of the world. It's good for his career, mind you. The image of an eccentric painter sailing the remote corners, bringing back masterpieces to show the rest of us the secrets of the wilderness—yes, that doesn't do any harm at all, but still I worry about the boy.'

Matthew, a boy? 'He seemed—er—fine. I'm sure—I really don't think you need worry.'

She had hung up, unable to suppress the thought that a man who could rouse such open fondness in his agent must have—well, he might understand things, might care. What if she were to take Shane to the west coast on their sailing trip? Not really looking for an old wooden sloop, of course, but simply sailing and leaving it up to fate.

Shane seemed indifferent to her plans.

'Mom, I'd rather stay here. I want to keep on at QC, flying and——'

'Shane, I——' She took a deep breath, wondering how much of this was a mother being selfish, but unwilling to give up the little bit of him that she had been counting on. 'Shane, in a few weeks you'll be gone to school. Before you go, I really feel that we should spend some time together.'

'I'll be back for Christmas. It's no big deal, Mom.'

She smiled, knowing she must not make him feel guilty for her own pain at his leaving, but determined enough to say, 'This isn't open for negotiation, honey.' She grinned, and he could not see any of the clinging she fought down. 'Look at it this way. It's a payment, the admission price you have to pay to go to school. Two weeks with your mother.'

There was a moment when she thought he might turn into rebellious fury, then he grinned wryly and said, 'Yeah, I guess I can do that.'

The next day she was on the seaplane dock in the early afternoon when Luke landed the twin-engine Goose on its scheduled flight from the mainland. When the Goose landed, she climbed down to help Luke with the small flurry of people and luggage.

'Where can I find a taxi?'

'Can you recommend a good hotel?'

'I was being met. Did you see a short, dark fellow in a yellow pick-up?'

The taxi came and went. The yellow truck turned up and took away two men with shiny suitcases. The couple with large backpacks grinned at Luke and hiked off in the direction of town.

There was only one woman left, standing a few steps away. A pretty, copper-haired woman, her hand linked tightly with the small, chubby fingers of a girl who might be five years old.

She was small and voluptuous enough to make Nicole feel ungainly and too tall, but her green eyes were filled with a tension that destroyed some of the beauty and brought lines to her face. This woman would be beautiful when the worry left her eyes, and she was strikingly unusual even with the sadness and tension radiating from her.

She was not one of the passengers who were terrified of flying, decided Nicole as she glanced at her curiously. The fear-of-flying people were usually not tense *after* the flight. It was more usual to see them sagging with the exhaustion of having kept the aeroplane in the air by force of their will.

'The Cessna get off?' Luke asked as he joined her on the float, his small pack dangling from his hand. She nodded and he asked, 'A flight to the Cape? Barry said it was urgent.'

She laughed then, forgetting the woman standing nearby. 'Oh, it was an emergency all right! The light-keeper ran out of tobacco. Apparently, as he explained to Barry on the radio-phone, he planned to quit smoking and deliberately let his supplies run down. Now he's regretting his decision, and he's desperate, will pay any price for a smoke.'

'You mean he's *chartering* a Cessna all the way down there just for a smoke? That's the best one I've heard all month!'

It was when their laughter faded that Luke remembered the woman waiting on the wharf, raised his hand and gestured her over. 'Nick, this is Roberta—and her daughter Anne. Roberta, this is Nicole Bentham, the pilot I told you about.'

The small woman stepped forward nervously, pulling the little girl along. The youngster's dark hair was long and straight, dark. Although Luke had introduced them as mother and daughter, there was little resemblance between them.

Roberta might be nervous, but her eyes were quick to go to Nicole's hand, to see the wedding ring before she spoke. 'Mrs Bentham, I'm so glad to meet you. Luke said you might be able to help me, that you would be able to recognise Matt's boat.' She had been smiling, smooth and polite despite the emotional lights in her eyes. Now her voice rose to desperation. 'I've just *got* to find him!'

Matt? She could only be talking about Matthew Kealy. From the swift concern on Luke's face, Nicole realised that her reaction must have been visible. She gasped desperately and managed to gather a cool mask around herself. No questions. No wondering. This woman was something to Matthew, probably his wife, and it must not matter to her.

She pulled her cap off and pushed a hand back through the blonde hair, freeing it and letting it tumble around her face. 'I don't exactly understand what you want, Mrs——?'

'I want to find Matt!' She spread her hands. The little girl beside her was silently tense, as if she might cry at a moment's notice. The mother said, 'Matthew Kealy. I want you to fly me to him. Luke said that you were out there, that you know where he is.'

'I know where he was a little over a week ago. I don't know where he is now.' Did she have to take this flight? Must she watch the joy in Matthew's face when he saw this Roberta with her wild mass of red hair and her small, soft, woman's curves?

'But you *could* find him,' insisted the woman, tossing the curls back, swallowing and transforming her face to a stubborn determination.

'Maybe.' It was the little girl that was her undoing. She had brown hair hauntingly like Matthew's, and she badly needed someone to hold her close and tell her the world would be all right. This was Matthew's child. She had his hair, his eyes, and she needed her father badly.

'All right,' she said finally. 'If Luke OKs it, we can go looking for him.'

'You could recognise the boat? You're sure?'

She shrugged, nodded. 'There aren't that many sail-boats on the west coast of the Charlottes.' She frowned at the woman. She was dressed for the city, high-heeled sandals and an elegantly tailored trouser suit that was never intended for the wilderness. 'I'm not sure if you realise what it's like out there. There are a lot of inlets, miles of nothing but trees and water, the odd fishing-boat. We can find him, eventually, but it's likely to be expensive for you to do it this way, and uncomfortable. Why don't you try raising him on the radio? The coast-guard has a network of radio repeaters. They should be able to raise him.'

She shook her copper head, clenched tighter on the girl's hands. 'He always turns the radio off.' She sounded desperate, as she might if there had been an argument, a separation, and she had to see him, to touch him, to get past the barriers, the resentments that might be there from the fighting. 'It doesn't matter what it costs! I just have to get to Matt! When can we leave?'

Nicole met Luke's eyes. He shrugged, indicated the Beaver. 'It's all set to go?' he asked her.

She nodded, said to Roberta, 'All right. We'll leave in ten minutes. You'd better go up to the office first and use the ladies room. We could be in the air a long time.'

Matthew's child. And that woman's. Roberta's. She did not want to find him in Security Cove, to see him take this woman in his arms in the same place where he had made love to her.

Roberta flew in the co-pilot's seat, her hands twisting together, her eyes staring blankly at the water below. Nicole flew over Security Cove and thankfully found it unoccupied, but went down for a closer look, just in case the trees might have fooled her, concealing *Charmaine*'s mast.

'Is this where he was?' Roberta shouted the question over the engine noise.

Nicole nodded. When they were in the air again, flying low over the water, taking the path a boat would, she was busy enough with watching that Roberta could not ask questions.

It was hard to communicate over the noise of the engine. Nicole could have given a set of headphones to Roberta, then they would have been able to talk easily over the intercom. She would have done that with most passengers, but she wanted to keep her distance from this woman, to try to tell herself this was an ordinary flight, a woman and a child being ferried out to meet a sail-boat.

The child was securely belted into a back seat, staring out the window, always looking down as if she too were searching for her father.

Did Mountain Man expect them?

When they had explored all the other nearby inlets, she lifted nose and increased throttle, climbing away towards the sea, heading south, watching for boats out to sea. Roberta pointed to an inlet to their left and Nicole shook her head.

'It's not charted. He wouldn't take his boat into an inlet without charts, would he?'

The redhead shrugged. 'I don't know. Maybe.'

She wanted this to be over. She wanted to be back home with Shane, to forget Matthew Kealy and the family she had not known he had. They could spend all day dodging in and out of places that no one but a maniac would take a boat. If he left Security Cove, she thought he would go to another secure anchorage, where he could paint and know that the boat would not be surging underfoot with the breakers from the sea.

He would be fascinated by the abandoned mine at Tasu, the open pit that had taken over the hillside until nature began to reclaim it. The old buildings were slated for demolition. They had stood abandoned for years now. He would want to get that on canvas, to paint the ruins of the mine and the village so that people could see what they had once been.

If he went up the hillside, painted a picture of the deer grazing on the new growth—if there were a picture like that, with the lines and depth that he had put into the painting she had seen half-finished on his easel, then she would go to him and ask if she could buy it.

She swallowed the pain. Perhaps they were divorced. Surely he was not a man who would wed a woman, then push her aside with lies while he played with another? With her, Nicole. God, no! How could she have let that happen? How could she do that to another woman?

'There's Tasu!' From the air it was a magic place. Whenever she approached she felt as if she were coming to another world, floating down on it from wide open ocean, seeing the narrow passageway that opened into a harbour that went for miles and miles. Stretching on, spreading out. God's green. A place to enfold you and tie your heart up, to tell you each day that you were part of a magical universe.

Roberta was not seeing the magic. She was twisting in her seat, shouting, 'I can't see any boats there. I—is that a town?'

The dock was behind the island, the old town site abandoned except for the caretaker. She brought the Beaver down, made a pass between the island town site and the abandoned mine site. Two fishing-boats. A power-boat of some kind, probably an old fishing-boat converted for pleasure. The mast of a sail-boat obscured by the big seine boat.

'I couldn't see anything!' complained Roberta. 'Was he there?'

She nodded and forced her heart to stop beating like a wild thing, concentrating on the routine. A complete circle, examination of the water for unexpected hazards. You could tear up floats, kill people, if you landed on a floating log. She had landed here only two weeks ago, but she was not about to trust it to be the same today.

Behind her a young voice called out, 'There he is! I see him! Mommy!'

No! She was not going to cry! She was going to make this the best landing she had ever done. Roberta Kealy was never going to know the instant they touched the water, and if Matthew was watching——

He was there, standing on the end of the dock. As she taxied slowly towards the old, deteriorating wharf she saw him moving a small boat that had been tied to the end of the float, making room for the plane to come in against the dock.

He could not know who was flying the Beaver, or who the passengers were. To Roberta she said brusquely, 'Stay in your seats until I've got it to the dock.' Then she swung the pilot's door open for better visibility and started manoeuvring into position.

Matthew caught the wing and gave her the thumbs up sign. She cut the engine and climbed out, in position to help her passengers down.

'Hello, angel.' His voice was low, a reminder of that night. She refused to look at him. 'I knew it was you when I saw the landing. No one but you can bring down a plane that gently.'

She felt an instant of pleasure, then she swallowed and said to the woman inside, 'OK, hand the baby down first, then you.'

The child seemed to fly into Matthew's arms, laughing and hugging tightly, her short arms squeezing hard around the man's muscular neck, an ecstatic reunion.

She had not jumped to any conclusions, had not made any mistakes. The child's high voice was saying, 'You're all scratchy! You've got a beard!' and the man was looking at her with eyes filled with love, saying, 'What do you think of it, sweetie? If you like it, I'll keep it.'

'Matt! Oh, darling, I've missed you so much!' Roberta stumbled as Nicole gave her a hand across to the dock, then she was the one in his arms, clinging tightly, saying, 'Oh, Matt, darling! I don't know how I've got by without you!'

She was crying, sobbing wildly against his chest. He—oh, it was there in his face. Nicole had to turn away, could not bear to see his eyes as he buried his face in the woman's red curls and tightened his arms around her. She tried not to hear his voice as she opened the luggage compartment and lifted out the single suitcase.

'Bobbie, honey,' he was murmuring. His hands would be in her hair, his voice all husky with love. 'Bobbie, take it easy. Don't cry, honey. It's going to be all right.'

'Oh, Matt!' she sobbed, the tears flowing as if he had started them fresh with his words. Nicole did not look, would not look, but she closed the luggage compartment and pushed off, watching the wing to be sure it would not hit anyone on the head as it slid away. Roberta's voice carried over the water. 'Matt, I've been so stupid. You told me, and I wouldn't listen. I don't know why you should be nice to me now—oh, Matt! Darling! You should be saying "I told you so".'

He laughed, a low, gentle sound. 'Bobbie, I would never tell you that any more than you would tell me what a God-awful mess I am, with six months' growth of hair everywhere.'

Roberta was dwarfed by the tall man, but her voice carried more clearly than his. 'You know, you're the only person I've ever let call me Bobbie.'

But that was his way, this Mountain Man. He called all his women by pet names. Sweetie for the little Anne, his daughter. Bobbie and honey for his wife. *Angel* for

Nicole, the woman who had spent one night in his arms, but she was not one of his women.

When she looked back they were tangled together like people who belonged. The tall, bearded man with one arm around the small, voluptuous beauty, holding tight while he bent to catch up the little girl with the long dark hair.

Nicole had no right to the feelings inside, to the pain wrenching as she watched him hold the beautiful redhead as if she were the only woman in his world. She hoped passionately that Roberta would never discover how faithless her man was.

And the little girl. What would that pretty little girl think if she knew her daddy had betrayed her mommy? That he had reached selfishly and taken what he wanted without even thinking of the people he was supposed to love.

How could Nicole have let herself be a party to this? She had always vowed never, *never* to get herself into a position where she could even be *thought* to come between a man and his wife.

The horrible thing was, even now, as she took off from Tasu, she actually felt sick at the thought of Matthew and the woman with the coppery curls making love with each other.

CHAPTER SIX

NICOLE was thankful when Luke gave her the job of tending to the film crew that was shooting near Masset. The moviemakers were demanding customers, sometimes infuriating and downright unreasonable; so she was far too busy ferrying temperamental film stars and arguing with foolhardy cameramen to think of the joyful reunion that was taking place aboard *Charmaine*.

Luke assigned Shane to her, to fetch and carry both messages and cargo, and she and Shane moved into a hotel in Masset for the duration of the assignment. She told herself she was happy that this small town on the north end of Graham Island was as far away from Tasu as you could get on these islands.

Shane loved his glimpse of the moviemaking industry, did not complain even when they worked from dawn to dark on the filming of one important scene.

The scene was to be shot from the Beaver. Nicole had a cameraman on board, Shane on the ground acting as a radio relay. When her son relayed that the director wanted the camera to come in *above* a stunt man climbing a rocky hillside, Nicole balked.

'You can't do that with a Beaver! There's a downdraft on that mountain. If I try to fly past there with my flaps on, we'll be on the rocks!' The cameraman beside her shrugged, but Nicole insisted, 'If you want that shot, get a helicopter.'

On the ground, the director grabbed Shane's radio and shouted, 'That shot has *got* to be done today!'

Later, Shane told her, 'He was hopping mad, Mom. He wanted to fire you, but you don't work for him. He got on radio telephone, got Luke at the base, but Luke said they had the best pilot in the company, and if they didn't like it they could take their business elsewhere.'

She felt a warm satisfaction at realising Luke valued her skills so highly, and was amazed to find that even her son seemed terribly proud of his mother. What had happened to Shane's sulky rebellion? He seemed mature and self-confident as he grinned and said, 'They can't get a helicopter up here for two days, so they're going to change the shot.'

If Matthew had not caught Shane stealing the magazine, dragged him off and confronted her with her son's behaviour, the boy might still be sulking and arguing, getting into far worse trouble.

The next day Nicole and the cameraman made the shot from the seaward side, not from above. Ironically, this was going to be the opening shot in the film, but it was the final camera shot they needed to wrap up the show.

The film-makers left and the islands returned to normal. Nicole and Shane were free for their promised two weeks' holiday. They flew back to Queen Charlotte and walked home together as the sun sank low on the horizon.

He was three steps ahead of her, going down the ramp to the floats, tossing back, 'You know, I think our sailing trip won't be too bad. I woulda liked to work for Luke 'til school starts, but he says if I want I can have a job next summer.'

She smiled and wanted badly to reach forward and touch his shoulder. She remembered just in time that public touching from mothers was not welcome to a fourteen-year-old man, and said merely, 'I'm going to miss you when you go to school.'

At the bottom of the ramp he stopped, turned back to her with a frown. 'Grandma said she'd like me to come for the holidays, and I know she—I don't really want to, but—well, I kind of owe it to her, don't I?'

Nicole pushed her hands deep into the pockets of her jeans. 'Why do you feel you owe it?'

'She's paying for the school, isn't she? That's the only thing that kind of bugs me, because——'

'She's not paying. I'm paying.' It was going to be hard, but all the hours of flying this summer would help. There was no way she would put her son in that woman's control.

'But Dad left the money for me, to——'

'In trust for you, in your grandmother's control.' She had left her cap at the base office as usual, but her hair was still tied back. Now she freed it, letting it wander around her shoulders. 'Some day it will be your money, but meanwhile I suggest you try to forget all about it.'

'Mostly I do.' He grinned and added, 'It's hard to think you're really rich when you're cleaning out planes where somebody got sick.'

She giggled, throwing the hair back and feeling really happy for the first time in a week. 'I'll bet it is!' She hoped he would grow up free of the attitude Tyler had had, that everything he wanted belonged to him.

Shane turned away, asking, 'We're leaving tomorrow, aren't we? Can we go out sailing on the west coast?'

She wished he had said the east, because Matthew was in the west, but right now there was nothing she could refuse this emerging man of hers. She smiled, trying to believe that this lanky, thin youth had once been small enough to hold in one arm, nursing at her breast. 'Why the west, Shane?'

'I dunno.' He squinted against the sun as it approached the hills on the other side of the harbour. 'I guess 'cause it's more adventurous. The east coast is so tame.'

'Tame?' She chuckled. 'All right. We'll go for the wild. We'll get provisions tomorrow, and check the tides. Then we'll go west through the narrows. We've got to go at high tide, and if you want *wild*, the passage through the narrows is about fifty feet wide, and——'

'As bent as a dog's hind leg?' When he tossed his shoulders back, he looked almost like her own father, although younger and fairer. Where was Tyler in him? 'Hey, Mom!' He was running now, his feet thudding on the wood. 'Hey! Look who's here!'

Oh, God! This Mountain Man was going to haunt her. She would never be free. There was *Charmaine*, her wooden mast just slipping through the entrance in the breakwater, and Shane shouting, 'Let's take their lines, help them dock.'

No. No way! What did Matthew need with them? He had Roberta, standing on the deck in shapely blue jeans, the lines in her hands. Shane could turn out if he wanted, but she was going into her boat, down below and out of sight.

She had trouble getting her key turned in the lock to her boat, finally got it opened just as *Charmaine*'s bowsprit approached the far side of this float. Well, at least he had no excuse for tying to *Island Wanderer* today! Salmon season was open and the wharfs were half-empty, all the fishing-boats gone out to sea.

She got out the tide tables, discovered that slack water in the narrows was early tomorrow afternoon. If she and Shane got up at first light, went for groceries, then fuel, they could be gone tomorrow. And west was perfectly safe now, because Matthew Kealy and his family were in Queen Charlotte City, hardly likely to go west again.

In fact, they were probably preparing to make the crossing to the mainland—and good riddance!

She was restless, needed something to do, but she had left everything immaculate the week before. She heard the companionway door swing open, heard the sounds of a man coming down. She knew who it would be.

She said bitterly, 'It's customary to knock, Mountain Man.'

There he was, tall enough that he had to bend his head slightly to stand in her companionway. 'I didn't know if you would answer, and I wanted to see you.'

Why was his voice so gentle? She felt a muscle spasm in her jaw. She was not going to look at him. Hearing him was too much. 'I don't want to talk to you.' She filled a kettle and put it on the gas. She had to have something to do. Miraculously, her hands were steady.

'Well——' He did not seem disturbed, just thoughtful.

She did not want to look at him. Roberta must have cut his hair. It would have been nice to think of her as a useless, hysterical female, but she obviously had a few talents, and she was not averse to helping dock a boat.

'You got your hair cut.'

He pushed his hands into his pockets. 'Yeah. Bobbie did it. Do you like it?'

She must have trimmed the beard, too. It was short and full. He looked terribly good, like a man who had wildness in him, but also culture and strength and romance. He looked like the kind of man any woman would be proud to call hers, and he belonged to the woman he called Bobbie.

'It doesn't matter what I think of it, does it?' She was proud of her voice, the coolness ringing around him with just a slight bite to it. As if she could care less about this man or his haircut. As if the whole thing made her feel slightly impatient.

'I think it does.' He was smiling, those eyes impossibly blue. 'That's why I wanted to talk to you, alone.'

Alone was the last thing they should be. She said with a tinge of desperation, 'Shane will be along any second.'

'No. I sent him up to show Anne where the store is. She's got two dollars and a burning urge to spend it.'

And where was the lovely Roberta? she wondered frantically. 'What right have you to send my son off to—— What are you doing here?' She stared at the kettle, but it would not boil for ages. 'Why are you on my boat, and what is it that you want to say?'

'In ten words or less?' His voice was wryly amused. 'Angel, the things that need saying between us can't be gone over that quickly.'

'*Nothing* needs saying!' She gulped, could not stop the rising of her voice. 'Whatever—it's done. I don't—you needn't worry that I'll tell her about what you—— Oh, damn it, Matthew Kealy! Will you just get out of my life?'

'You're sputtering, and you're not making any sense at all. Why are you so upset?'

'Upset? Shut up! Get out!' The water boiled, spurting out of the spout of the over-filled kettle, making her leap back to avoid the boiling splash. 'Damn! See what you've done? No, don't touch me!'

But he was, his fingers on her shoulder, his other hand turning off the gas. He was far too close. She wailed, 'Oh, Matthew! What are you doing here? Go away! Please!'

'I tried that.' His eyes were an angry blue fire. 'We started something out there in Security Cove. I think we've got to finish it, angel.'

'Finish...' How could anyone have this kind of power over her? She wanted to melt into his arms. Just his fingers touching her shoulder, and she was putty, melting butter, all the soft things with no will-power. Her voice was as weak as the rest of her. 'Matthew, I—are you—what do you want? An affair with me?'

His fingers brushed her cheek, threaded through her hair as he moved it softly behind her shoulders. His voice was bemused. She was unwillingly fascinated, her lips parting and seeing his eyes watching. 'Angel, we already started the affair. I think——' She saw the movement of his closely trimmed beard as he swallowed, then his voice was even huskier. 'It might be a long time before this affair is over.'

She pulled back, sick that she could want him so much, be so close to flinging herself into his arms when his wife was waiting only yards away. She came up against her gas stove, spread her hands behind her.

She gulped, said desperately, 'It's a good thing you've got such a good memory, isn't it?' Why could she not feel the icy anger in her voice? 'The newspapers. That's what I'm talking about. Some women might hesitate to have an affair with a man like you, but you know better, don't you? You know all about me.'

He stepped closer and she had nowhere to go. 'Angel, we should talk about that. It's a little hard to explain, but when I read that newspaper article I——'

'Oh, I understand! I know all about it. I had a good teacher, so don't bother trying smooth words!' It was getting easier, Tyler's memory fuelling her anger. 'Oh, I know how it goes! "You'd just like a little something on the side." It doesn't mean anything to you that you're married, that there's a woman who thinks you're going to be faithful to her?'

He jerked. 'Hey, angel, slow down! You——'

'No! Will you stop calling me that? I'm not your angel! I—you had no right to do what you did to me out there in Security Cove. You had no right to involve me in that kind of a——'

His hands grasped her shoulders, his lips descending on hers. It was wrong, terribly wrong, but she opened her mouth to him, allowed his tongue to plunder the depths of her, to reduce her to a shuddering softness pressed against his muscular chest.

Passion flared in her as if it had never died, but had lain banked, waiting for this man's touch. Just a gentle probing of the softness of her mouth, the soft caress of fingers along her bare arms. Then he grasped her wrists and pulled them gently up, and she wound her arms around his neck and lost control of all reason.

Warm hands against her back, moulding her against the solid maleness of Matthew. Her fingers tracing the rigid cords of his neck, threading through the short, soft hairs of his beard, feeling him trembling from her touch. Then his lips pulled away from hers, caressed the softness of her cheek and her neck, nibbled at the tenderness of her earlobe.

Outside, a light voice called out, 'Matt?'

Nicole froze, passion and feeling draining away abruptly. 'You'd better go back to her, hadn't you?' She jerked her arms away from his face. 'Back to your *wife*!' she said harshly. 'You're not really getting anywhere here. That's all you're getting—just that kiss. I do *not* want an affair with you! I don't believe in extra-marital affairs, and I won't be——'

She gulped. His hands were still holding her. She had nowhere to go, no room to back away. 'Let go of me, Matthew. You're not going to be my lover. Not ever.'

His eyes held the memory and she gulped, 'Never again.'

'You don't want me to be unfaithful to Bobbie?' He looked almost ready to laugh, and she felt fury. How could she want a man who would do this?

'That's right,' she agreed tightly. 'I don't want anything to do with you.'

He shook his head. 'I have trouble believing that.' His fingers brushed the swelling of one of her breasts, his eyes noting her reaction. He whispered, 'You know it's not true, and I know it. Angel, there's no need to worry about Bobbie. She wouldn't object, and——'

'Damn! Will you get the hell out of here?' She covered her ears with her hands, said frantically, 'I do not want to hear your lies! Go and mess up your marriage on your own. I'm not helping!'

'Listen, angel.' His hand grasped her arm and she jerked back, then somehow managed to push past him. She pointed furiously at the companionway even while he tried to say, 'If you'll just listen for a minute, I can explain everything...'

She shut her eyes painfully. 'Do you know how often I have heard that? You can explain, can you? Oh, I'll just bet you can, but I don't want to hear it. It's going to be all lies, and I've had enough bloody lies to last me a lifetime! Right now, all I want is for you to get out of here and never come back!'

She opened her eyes and found him still there. She stepped back, said coldly, 'I do not want you here! I don't want you——' His eyes flashed and she remembered his touch too well, changed it to, 'Sure, I'm physically attracted to you, but I do not *want* to want you. All I want is never to see you again. And *please* stop calling me *angel*!' She heard the voice outside, said tiredly, 'She's calling you again.'

He shook his head, said gently, 'It's not over, angel. I'll be back—tomorrow, when you're calmer.'

She shook her head silently, then found herself alone and trying to pretend that tears were not flowing down her cheeks.

She would *not* see him tomorrow!

She spent the evening getting shipshape, checking her food stores and making a list of what was needed. Shane had deserted her and she knew he was on *Charmaine*. She was not about to interfere. Getting Shane home to help with the work of preparing for their holiday would mean talking to either Matthew or his wife. She could not face that.

But Shane was smiling when he came home, and she hated refusing him when he said, 'Mom, couldn't we hang around here for a couple of days? Matt said he'd look at my sketches.'

She shook her head. 'Take the sketches over in the morning while I'm shopping,' she said finally. 'We're setting sail on the afternoon tide.'

'But tomorrow Roberta is——'

'Shane!' He was staring at her, bewildered because she never shouted. She got herself under control and said tightly, 'Shane, I do not want to talk about Roberta or—or Matthew. I know you like him, but—please don't talk to me about him.'

He was plainly bewildered. 'But Mom——'

Damn! The tears were threatening again, and she could not remember crying since her father's death. 'Honey, I know it doesn't make sense to you, but please just do as I want on this. And please don't ask a lot of questions.'

CHAPTER SEVEN

NICOLE and Shane spent their first night in a sheltered anchorage just west of the channel that ran between the north and south island, beachcombing and relaxing. She was soaking up the feeling of being in a place that might have been the end of the world.

Shane wanted to dig clams, but Nicole vetoed the idea. 'Remember the two women Luke flew out of here two years ago? They'd roasted clams, and the next thing they were unconscious.'

'Red Tide,' said Shane, half remembering the incident.

'Paralytic shellfish poisoning,' corrected Nicole automatically.

'Same thing. Everyone calls it Red Tide. But if it was here two years ago, there's no reason to expect it here now.' He was right, of course, but there was no way she could eat clams from this anchorage when the memory of that emergency flight was so clear in her mind.

When they rowed the dinghy back out to their boat, they pored over the charts. Shane traced his finger southwards, 'What about this cove here for an anchorage tomorrow night? Security Cove. Well sheltered. Mud bottom, so it'll be good holding ground for the anchor.'

He sounded so mature, like a man planning their trip, but she could not possibly lie at anchor in the place where Matthew had found his way through all the inhibitions that bound her in one short night. She looked at the chart, but there was nowhere else within a day's sail; only the uncharted bays that were so common on the remote west coast.

'Why don't we try something adventurous, Shane? We could sail out in the morning, head right out to sea, make a long tack down to . . . there—Tasu. We'd have to be out overnight.'

She was glad they did it that way; not only because she escaped the memories at Security Cove, but also because of the peace that came to her on the long overnight passage. She and Shane alternated watches through the dark hours, and she found the night-time ocean filled with a surging exhilaration not unlike a flight high over the mountains.

In Tasu, Shane brought out his sketch-book and they went exploring the abandoned town and the old mine. They climbed the hills behind the mine, taking their lunch with them and making a day of it, returning to their boat shortly before sunset. The next day they went climbing again.

On the second day, a small deer emerged from the bush near Nicole while Shane was sketching on the other side of the clearing. She held her breath as it approached, afraid of frightening the wild creature.

The wind was in her face. The deer came within a foot of her before smelling human scent. Then it stopped, arrested, staring at her in a moment's silent communication. Then it was gone, gently trotting out of the clearing without any evidence of fear or panic.

'Mom, stay there! Don't move!'

She stood for a long time at the edge of the hillside while Shane tried to recreate, on paper, the sight of his mother with the deer. He tried again the next day, finally giving up, muttering, 'I wish the deer would come back again. There's something wrong with the way I've drawn it. I wish I could ask Matt about it.'

That day, and the next, Shane worked on sketching nature's reclamation of the mine. Nicole simply relaxed on the hillside. She felt as if she could lie in the sun for ever. When she opened her eyes, she could look down over the large harbour of Tasu with its arms of water. Without moving anything but her head, she could even watch the narrow passage that led from the sea.

How many days had they been here? The sun moved across the sky every day, but time was suspended for her until the morning when she looked down on a sail-boat's mast emerging from the rocky entrance.

Charmaine. Matthew.

Her heart stopped.

The sloop raised sail once inside the narrow entrance, catching the light winds. For a few minutes, she thought he might be going up the north arm of the harbour, but then *Charmaine* came back on the second tack and slipped behind the island town site.

Luckily she and Shane had brought their lunch. They need not go back down to the town for hours yet, and it would take her that long to prepare for this. But it was all right. She was going to see him this evening on her return, and it would not matter any more than—well, than seeing an old flame.

Actually, she had very little experience with old flames. She had married her first love at eighteen, and until Matthew Kealy no one else had touched her heart. But it did not matter that Matt was down there. It was inevitable, really. With her flying around the islands, and him sailing, they were bound to encounter each other again and again.

With Roberta? Surely the vivacious woman was not a creature of the sea, ready to live her life beyond the edge of civilisation?

Behind her, Shane said, 'What do you see?'

He would be glad to find Matt at the wharf when they came down the hill tonight, but she was not ready yet.

She said, 'Just the harbour. Light on the water,' and he bent his head over the pad again. 'Shane, did you show Mr Kealy your sketches?'

He nodded. She waited, but there was only silence. She hoped that Matthew had not hurt Shane with harsh criticism. She would have trouble forgiving him if he had done that.

What was she thinking? Forgive a man who had used her to be unfaithful to the beautiful Roberta? What kind of a person was she, if her ethics could erode as swiftly as a man's warm gaze touched her skin? She shivered and almost wondered if she should not have understood Tyler's weaknesses more.

'Did he say anything about the sketches?'

Shane concentrated on the movement of his hand over the paper, watched the horizon. Lord, he looked a bit like Matthew when he did that. She had not wanted to watch Mountain Man as he worked at his easel in the cockpit, but the image of him working must have soaked into her subconscious.

It would have been wonderful for Shane to have a chance to learn from an artist like Matthew. If only——

Her nemesis. Was that what Matthew was? Her fate, because she had condemned Tyler for his endless casual affairs, and now she was to discover what it was that made a person forget everything but the need to touch, to love.

Maybe they were divorced. Roberta had come back, but perhaps he did not want her back. Oh, how could she be wishing unhappiness on Roberta because she wanted—— It could never be more than an affair, a sexual interlude, and she damned well would not let herself be drawn into casual sex!

And she would not cry!

* * *

'I thought you didn't do portraits?'

That was Bobbie's voice, echoing in his memory as he climbed the hill with Anne on his shoulders.

Bobbie had been searching the boat for her suitcase while he coached Anne through a picture-book, and Matt hadn't thought that she might go into the aft cabin where he stored his paintings. He and Anne had progressed to the zebras by the time Bobbie returned with the suitcase and the question.

'I thought you didn't do portraits?' Her voice contained the disturbing quality that meant she intended to get to the bottom of something.

He had shrugged, said evasively. 'Sometimes, if there's something special.'

Something special. He had called her *angel*, but she was no angel. He remembered the newspaper. These days it was hard to keep remembering the newspaper article, but easy to remember the impact that picture had made.

He had been walking down Granville Street in Vancouver, high with the success of his first showing at Lyndon's gallery. He had stopped in mid-stride when he saw her picture in one of those newspaper machines. Just newsprint, but all soft and...her hair, her eyes...soft and strong at the same time, the kind of woman he would—— Well, it had been only an illusion. All he had to do was read the newspaper article to know that.

Reading the article, learning about her with his mind still yearning from that fantasy her picture had created... He had felt hurt, defensive, almost as if it were Matthew Kealy that she had betrayed. He had thrown the newspaper angrily into a bin, had managed to push the thing far enough back in his mind so that when he saw her again, he wasn't sure where he remembered her from.

Nicole. He had tried to paint her as she was in his mind, to escape the haunting image by transferring it to canvas. It had felt like the kind of obsession that he could only escape by painting it.

Bobbie, standing in the wheelhouse, had placed her fists on her hips, determined. 'I saw the painting you've got drying back there. I think she's—you——'

He had said, 'I hardly know her,' but it did not feel true. Then Bobbie had left, packing her suitcase and flying away on the jet, leaving Anne behind with him.

And Matt had set sail immediately, heading west, searching for a sleek fibreglass sailing-ship.

He had to exorcise her. The word sounded ludicrous, but it was nothing more than the truth. He could not paint, could not think of anything except the blonde angel in the painting, the woman he would have liked her to be.

Damn! If he had never seen that newspaper he would have sworn that he had painted the woman she was. How could anyone with those eyes be a tramp?

Luckily Anne was willing to go anywhere. She liked sitting in the high chair in the wheelhouse and watching the waves ahead of them. She had no idea that they were looking for a needle in a haystack.

In his arms in Security Cove, the angel had been a woman hungry for love, giving as much as she received, seeming horrified by her abandon when morning came—as if it were something she had never done before.

At night, when Anne was sleeping in the short bunk beside the stove, he went into the aft cabin and stared at the canvas that his mind had titled *Portrait of an Angel*.

Nicole, lying with the covers twisted around her, her hair a fine golden halo spread out over the pillows. She was warm and real and innocent, but her eyes were heavy with a woman's passion, and her lips were parted for the man she loved. A woman who had been untouched, now passionate and vulnerable for the one man who held the key to her heart.

It hurt him every time he looked at it. He wished he had never painted it, yet he could not leave it alone, any more than he could leave her alone.

Searching this wild west coast was almost hopeless, unless you knew the skipper you were looking for. This lady would not be a foolhardy sailor. Sensible. Practical. Except when she was in his arms, or—no, he must not think too much about that!

Northerly winds, so the south was a better bet. And Shane had mentioned going to see Anthony Island. That was two votes for the south. She would not go to Security Cove, but he checked it anyway. In the cove, Anne saw the long grass of the delta on shore and wanted to go exploring.

'Sorry, sweetie, but not today.' He hauled some ice-cream out of the freezer to distract her, then put her to bed to sleep while he motored out of Security Cove and around Inskip Channel in the dark, using his radar to navigate and watching for anchor lights in the bays he passed. He was certain that she would not anchor without a light. She obeyed the safety rules.

But that didn't make sense, did it? The woman described in the newspaper had not been like that, she had been reckless and wild and...and she had been Nicole Bentham.

Anne was colouring in a book she had brought with her when they came out of the big ocean swell into Tasu Sound. He put the sails up once they were inside, and with the sun beating down on them he felt a surge of happiness that was almost painful.

She was here. He saw her tall mast as he sailed around the end of the island where the town site was built. He tied up, noting that the lock was on the door of *Island*

Wanderer, saying to Anne, 'OK, sweetheart, let's go for that walk you wanted.'

He took the binoculars and, unusual for him, did not take his sketching-pad. Predictably, Anne was tired by the time they had climbed the tree-lined road from the town to the causeway. He lifted her on to his shoulders and she rode there, her hands sometimes laced through his hair, and sometimes locked around his throat.

Anne asked, 'Where are the people?' as they climbed the steep road to the mine buildings.

'Gone.' He was walking quickly, although he could feel the nervousness growing inside himself. 'The owners closed the mine and the people all had to move away.'

'Nobody left?'

'Only the caretaker.' She was either thinking hard about that, or had decided to concentrate on something else. He climbed silently through the collection of old, empty buildings and out on to the access road that led around the big open pit of the abandoned mine.

He set her down and used the binoculars to search the hillside. He saw two deer standing on the edge of a cliff, but he almost missed the woman leaning against a rock on the outcropping above the deer. He would have moved his search on, passing the brown of her jacket, but the sun caught the gold of her hair and he found her.

His heart stopped, then slammed hard against his ribs. 'Hop back up, sweetheart.' His voice was hoarse, almost breathless. 'We're going up the hill.'

'I'm thirsty,' she complained.

'We'll find a creek and you can drink there.'

She stared at him, the beginnings of rebellion around her mouth. He found himself wondering how much trouble Bobbie had handling this child who usually looked so docile.

'I don't want to,' she insisted petulantly.

'Well, you can ride, or you can walk, but you're coming up the hill.' She stared at him for almost a minute, then he was amazed to see her lips quirk with a suppressed smile as she came close.

'Lift me up, please, Uncle Matt.'

He thought Nicole might have moved before he got there. It could be hard to find her on this overgrown hillside if she went into the trees. It would probably have made more sense to wait for her to come back to her boat.

He had not wanted to wait.

He had wanted that moment before she saw him, to watch her while she did not know anyone was there. Perhaps he hoped to discover which woman she was—the one in his painting, or the one in the newspaper.

She had been angry, believing that he was married when he'd made love to her. The woman in the newspaper would not have cared, would she?

When he came out into the clearing, he found Shane at the edge of the trees, a sketch-pad on his knee. Nicole was there, too, still lying against the rock. She saw him, but there was no sign of surprise, no reaction at all. He moved to Shane, not quite ready to contend with the look in the angel's eyes.

Shane tensed a little as he came close, so Matt stopped and asked, 'Mind if I look?' The boy held out the pad. Matt studied it until Shane said hesitantly, 'I know something's wrong, but I can't seem to figure it out.'

'It's perspective. Work on this line——' He traced his fingers lightly over the paper. 'The rest is good—catches a mood of other-worldliness. I like it.'

Shane sat straighter. Anne was twisting on Matt's shoulders, eager to get down. The boy grinned at Anne while saying to Matt, 'I've been working on my perspective, like you said the other day. It's hard.'

Matt grinned. 'Don't I know it! But you've improved, even in these few days. What you want is a couple of years of art school, to learn all the tricks and decide which ones suit you.' He reached up and lifted the squirming girl over his head. 'Meanwhile, do you think I could get you to take this young lady and find her a stream? She's thirsty.'

Nicole had not moved. He crossed the clearing, dropped down near her, sitting cross-legged on the grass. He watched her profile as she stared down at the water. 'Why are you here?' she asked finally.

'Looking for you.' He saw her swallow, knew that she felt the same unwilling pull he did.

'Where's your wife?'

She would not look at him, but if he leaned closer he could touch the soft curtain of her hair.

'My wife?' He shook his head, but she did not look. '*Bobbie*'s gone home. She left on the plane the same day you went through the narrows.' She looked at him, startled, and he saw a million questions in her eyes before she looked away, concentrating on a blade of grass that her fingers had found. 'Angel, Bobbie is not my wife, she's my twin sister.'

'Your——' That brought the eyes to him, but they were wide and sceptical. 'She doesn't look anything like you.'

'I know.' He resisted the urge to touch, afraid to drive her away. 'Fraternal twins aren't really any closer related than ordinary brothers and sisters. Bobbie takes after our mother. I'm more like Dad, long and skinny.'

She was unwillingly fascinated, although nervous of believing him too easily. He was a man her soul seemed to know, but a stranger regardless. 'Does your father have a beard, too?'

'Nope.' He grinned. 'My father never did anything unconventional in his life. For that matter, I don't usually have a beard either. I misplaced my razor and, living out here, it didn't seem to matter if I bothered replacing it. Look, if you don't believe me about Bobbie, you can look at my pictures back on the boat. I've got an album. There's a picture of our joint first birthday party, and her hair was red then, too.'

Her eyes were drawn up the hillside. 'Anne's your niece?' She pushed her hair back, her mouth troubled. 'But if that's so, why didn't she go home with her mother?'

'Her mother's got problems.' He frowned, said, 'Bobbie married Henry ten years ago. I tried to warn her, but—she wasn't listening to advice, and I probably wasn't very tactful at giving it. But Henry had all the signs of an alcoholic when she met him, and he's the kind of guy who thinks his woman should exist for only one purpose: to idolise him. If anything, he's got worse in the last ten years.

'The explosion came last month. Bobbie was offered a job at one of the Vancouver radio stations, and he forbade her to take it.' He grinned, although she could still see the worry in his eyes. 'I could have told him that was no way to handle Bobbie. She's taken so much from him, but I guess that was the catalyst that convinced her she had to leave him. I don't know if they'll get back together. Right now they're working on World War Three. Henry's threatening to take Anne from her, and Bobbie's afraid he might kidnap her and disappear.'

'Would he?' She shivered, remembering when she had confronted Tyler with the demand that they separate.

'I don't know, but I don't want Anne in the middle of their fight. Bobbie came here to ask me if I could take Anne and keep her safe, keep her out of all the fighting, until things cool down.'

Anne's young laughter rang out as she started running with Shane along the ridge above. Matthew said, 'She thinks it's just a holiday.'

Nicole said softly, 'I'm glad you took her. I wouldn't want her torn up in a custody battle.'

He was frowning, saying, "I don't think any sane judge would give Henry custody.'

She thought of Tyler, of the cases he had taken and won, for money rather than because he believed in them. 'It depends,' she said bitterly. 'If he has a sharp lawyer——'

'No. She'll have the best legal advice there is in Vancouver, and if it looks bad, I can go down and testify. I'd prefer not to, but I can assure you that no one will award custody to Henry if I go on the stand.'

He looked grim and she wondered what he knew about his brother-in-law. Then he seemed to shake it off, turning to her and saying softly, 'That's not why I came here, to talk about Bobbie's problems.'

Her heart stopped. 'Why? Why did you follow me?'

'To finish what we started.'

She shook her head, pulling back against the rock although he had not made a move to touch her. He reached a hand towards her then and she shook her head, her eyes holding that frightened skittishness he had seen before.

'Nicole——'

'Don't! Please, Matthew, I—I don't want this.' She pushed back her hair and his eyes followed her motion. Her hand froze on the long, soft strands.

He shifted closer, but he could feel her tension. He touched the crease above her eyes, softly smoothing it. His fingers traced down the curve of her cheekbone to the tremulous vulnerability of her lips. 'You want what I want,' he whispered.

She jerked away, stumbling to her feet, stepping back. 'No! I—stay away from me.' She was breathing heavily. She pushed her hands into her jeans pockets as if she did not know what else to do with them.

'What do you think I'm going to do to you?' He was on his feet too, now, raking his hands through his hair. He knew that if only he could get her in his arms, she would tremble and respond to him. He wanted terribly to touch her, hold her, feel the warmth of her, but it was not enough.

He wanted her to come into his arms willingly. He said softly, 'Angel, I want you. You know that. I've never wanted another woman the way I want you, but I'm not about to force myself on you.' He jerked his head back, indicating the bank overhead. 'You needn't worry. I'm not going to try anything with your son and my niece only a few feet away.'

He could see her throat move as she swallowed, but she didn't speak and he said softly, 'We could spend time here, get to know each other. Shane's going to school in a couple of weeks, isn't he?' She nodded, her eyes watching his, but her face blank. 'Anne will be going home about the same time, I expect. Bobbie won't want her to miss school. She starts grade one this year.'

'What——?' She pushed the hair back again, but it would not stay. The wind caught it and spun gold around her face and shoulders. It hurt, thinking of Shane going. She wished she could stop time, keep him here for ever.

'Once the children are gone, we could pick up where we left off.' He did not move any closer, but she felt the pressure of his closeness. 'We've started something we can't just leave, angel.'

'I didn't—I don't——' She swallowed, and wondered if she had the strength to push him away if he touched her. When he had come out of the trees, sitting carefully near her and talking about his sister, she had felt something warm and powerful growing inside. But he was a man who wanted only an affair, while she was a woman who knew better than to trust any man. She said weakly, 'I'm afraid you're out of luck, Mountain Man. Whatever you may have read in the newspaper, I'm not the kind of woman who indulges in casual sex.'

He must have seen something in the mask that was her face. He said, 'Nicole, I——'

She pleaded, 'Will you please just get out of here? Leave me alone and——'

'I'm sorry.'

He sounded angry, not sorry. He spun around and started to pace away, but he could not leave her like this. He came back, his eyes penetrating, probing. She was like a frightened child, not a sophisticated woman.

For a long moment they stared at each other, then he said very softly, 'He hurt you a lot, didn't he?'

She jerked, shook her head. 'What do you mean?'

'Tyler Bentham. Your late husband.'

She shivered, then seemed to firm into a cool disdain. 'I don't know what you're talking about.' Then the mask collapsed. She swallowed and got out words that might make a barrier to stop him, to hide from that gentle something in his eyes. 'You read it in the paper. You've got all the answers.' Her voice was rising, losing conviction. 'Tyler didn't hurt me. We had that kind of marriage. He was f-free to do what he wanted. So was I.'

The words echoed senselessly around them, fading to silence. He could see the high flush on her cheeks, the pain in her eyes, and he knew the truth. 'I don't believe that. I don't believe you were up north having an affair when Tyler died. Where were you, angel? Why didn't you go to the funeral?'

She seemed to explode, stamping close to him and shaking that beautiful mane of fair hair in a cloud around her shoulders. 'You're another one, aren't you? Artist, hell! You'd think you had eyes of your own, could look at things and make up your mind for yourself! Oh, no! You're just like everyone else! You read something in the damned newspaper and it's bloody gospel truth! Well, Matthew bloody Kealy, you can take your damn—your *truth* and—and——'

She seemed to collapse against the rock, leaning into it for support. He reached her, had to hold her in his arms because she was trembling too much to stand alone and she needed him.

He rocked her gently, almost as if she were a child, murmuring soothing noises against her hair, sounds that slowly developed into words. 'Don't cry, angel. It's all right.' He kissed her eyes where the faint dampness betrayed her inner turmoil. 'I know you weren't the woman they wrote about in the newspaper.'

She choked, 'You said——'

He held her tighter. 'I said a lot of damned fool things. The woman I met in Queen Charlotte—the woman I made love to in Security Cove wasn't—angels don't behave the way they said you did in that newspaper article.'

She almost laughed, choking over the tears. 'Matthew, I was no angel in Security Cove. I—you've got to believe me, but I've never behaved like that in my life before.'

He smoothed her hair back, carefully brushed the damp tendrils that were clinging to her face. 'I knew it then, that what we had was special, but when I remembered that newspaper I—angel, you're going to have to tell me about it.'

She shook her head, not wanting to bring it all back again. He seemed to understand her unwillingness, but he said softly, 'Just once, angel. I have to know, and then we can forget it all.'

He took her with him, down to the soft grass, cradling her in his arms as if it were a safe place for ever. She protested weakly, 'Shane... Anne...'

He brushed her words aside. 'They're way up the hill.'

She gave up then, closed her eyes and let herself enjoy the security of his arms, and finally she told him.

She had been seventeen when she had met Tyler, a girl newly graduated, having lived all her life in the remote north coast town of Kemano. 'You can't get there by road,' she told him. 'There's just a town site of about three hundred, the workers at the power plant, and a boat from outside a couple of times a week. My father had a seaplane, though, and we went in and out as we pleased on his days off.'

She had stayed in Kemano, taking her schooling by correspondence while most of the other children went out to the city for high school. Her father had not wanted to let her go, and she had always chosen to be with him above all others.

'I was an only child, and more than that, because my mother died when I was small. I went everywhere with him. He flew, so I flew. I had my pilot's licence before I graduated. Then, when I went out to university, the world hit me like an explosion.'

Tyler had been the first, the only one. A law student, handsome and wealthy enough to take her riding in fast cars, partying to soft music and low lighting. She had been swept off her feet, adoring the dark man who had mysteriously chosen her as the girl he most wanted to be with.

She felt Matthew's arms close around her, said slowly, 'I was terribly inexperienced, and I thought I had found the only man in the world, that I could trust him for a lifetime. I never could figure out what he saw in me.' The memories were strong as she said, 'When he learned I was pregnant, it was quite a shock to him.'

But Tyler had done the honourable thing. 'They had to make me over,' she told Matthew dully. 'Tyler and his mother. I couldn't do anything right. I didn't dress right, or walk right, or talk right. I had to be a lawyer's wife, and Mrs Bentham told me that one day Tyler was going to be a politician. It didn't matter. I loved him, and I would have done almost anything.'

Matthew said, 'I know what he saw in you.'

She shook her head. 'It was hard for me, but there was Shane coming and I tried to tell myself I would see more of Tyler once he was established in the law firm.' She shrugged. 'But then the political games started. He was running for a seat in the provincial government, and it was—I hated it. I went to the parties...the lunches...the speeches with Tyler talking and me standing at his side. He seemed to be growing farther and farther away. I never saw him. I—oh, damn, Matthew! I did love him, and I spent so many nights waiting, hoping he would come home to me.'

He smoothed her hair back, held her head against his shoulder so that she could feel the deep, steady beat of his heart before he asked, 'When did you realise he was seeing other women?'

She shuddered, remembering the night Shane had fallen from the fence in the back garden. 'He was only four, and he looked so helpless lying in that ambulance stretcher. In the hospital, they weren't sure at first if there was a fracture. Then they found there was, and I couldn't find Tyler anywhere. It was in the middle of the campaign, and I called everyone I could think of, except his campaign manager, because she had an unlisted phone and I didn't know the number.'

She would have stayed at the hospital all night, but the doctor had finally sent her away and told her there was nothing to do but wait, that she should sleep. 'God, Matthew! I was so terribly worried. I was afraid my baby was going to die.'

He kissed her, said softly, 'I wish I had been there for you.' If he had been, his arms would have been around her like this.

'I've never felt so alone. I found Tyler. When I left the hospital I went to the campaign manager's apartment, and he answered the door. There was really no doubt, even for someone as stupidly trusting as me. She was his mistress. I guess she had been for a long time.'

The wind came up and swept up the long hill, stirring her hair and bringing her back to the present, to Matthew's arms around her and the children's voices echoing from somewhere above. She pushed herself away, and his arms released her.

'He said it had never happened before, and it never would again. That he loved me, and—I tried to believe it, but it wasn't true. I think he was unfaithful to me from the first, and it hurt more because I had believed in him, trusted him. It took me a long time, four more years, but in the end I knew it would never change. I never saw him except for the political requirements. Mostly I saw his mother, because we lived in her house. It was the family house, and she kept a close eye on me to be sure I was being a good Bentham wife, saying the right things and having the right friends, wearing the right clothes. I used to escape to the flying field. When Shane went to school, I joined the flying club. I spent a lot of my afternoons in the air. It made the rest of it easier to take.' She smiled a little sadly, said, 'You know, the funny thing was, I still loved him. I couldn't stand to live with him, couldn't trust him any more, but I still cared about him.'

His arms tensed. 'Couldn't live with him? The newspaper didn't mention a separation.' He was sure of that.

'No one knew, just Tyler and I and—and Mrs Bentham.' She pushed the hair back. Matthew was very still, listening with both his ears and his eyes. 'He won that first election, then our social life became terrible, the trivial things so important. When the Minister Tyler was cultivating expressed an interest in sailing, Tyler had to have a sail-boat to invite him sailing. When the Minister said he wanted to see the Queen Charlotte Islands, Tyler had the boat delivered up here, and we flew north for sporadic visits when we had important guests. The next summer, when the first sailing trip was over, Tyler went back, but Shane and I stayed.' Matthew said nothing and she said defensively, 'I liked it up here, and we simply stayed.'

He shook his head. 'It took more than that. Something happened. What was it?'

She shrugged, said, 'Nothing new. He had an affair with the Minister's wife and it—I just couldn't handle it any more. He always promised me, said it was nothing, that he loved me, and—I kept believing, trying to believe. Then I—I just reached the point where I couldn't believe it any more.'

'So you stayed? He didn't fight it?' Matt thought he knew better. He knew the kind of lawyers who played politics.

'Yes, he fought it! He—he didn't want me to stay up here. Election time was coming up again, and politics mattered more to him than anything else. A separation, or a divorce, isn't good campaign material.' She sat up away from him, her voice cold in spite of the trembling. 'I never thought I was a hard person, but I was hard then. I made a deal with him, forced him because he couldn't fight with the election coming up.'

'You made him give you the boat.'

She stared at him. 'Yes. I told him I would fly down for the important events, but only the most important. But I was staying up north, with Shane, and he had to sign over the boat to me. If he didn't agree, I was going to file a divorce suit against him, and name the Minister's wife as co-respondent.'

Tyler had had no choice but to accept. At one point she had almost weakened in her resolve to take the boat, but she had had few resources of her own, and she'd needed the boat as a home for Shane.

'And there was no other man for you, was there?' He knew that now, but somehow he had to have the words.

'No. The man in the newspaper stories was William Stewart—my father. When Tyler was in that car accident, I was in Kitimat, at the hospital with my father. There's no hospital in Kemano, so they flew my father out to Kitimat when he had a heart attack, and they thought he was going to make it.

'I was with him for a week. Two days after I arrived, Tyler was killed in the accident with that actress. I would have gone to the funeral. I really never could hate him, despite all that happened, but I couldn't leave Dad. He—the doctors were saying it was going to be all right, but then he had another attack and... he never made it. I never made it to Tyler's funeral, nor did Shane. I saw the newspapers, afterwards. Mrs Bentham cut out the relevant articles and sent them to me later.'

Matthew said tightly, 'You should have forced them to print a retraction. Some reporter should have been kicked out of the profession. Saying things like that without a shred of evidence. Do you realise what a case you would have had against the newspaper in a court of law?'

She shivered. 'You talk like a lawyer. The last thing I wanted was to have my private life dragged through the law courts.'

CHAPTER EIGHT

SHE was up early the next morning, out on deck and watching the sky. All bright, dark blue, with a few white clouds moving fast over the hilltops. Northerly winds. Good sailing.

She watched the clouds moving, knowing that she should leave, sail away while she could; yet inside acknowledging a strong desire to stay, climb the hills up almost to the sky, knowing that Matthew was nearby. Her awareness of him was so intense that when she turned away from her perusal of the sky and the hills, she felt no sense of surprise when her eyes travelled over the stern of *Charmaine*, to the roomy cockpit, the man leaning back in a chair in the corner, a cup of coffee in his hand and a half-smile on his lips. She had never thought much about beards, but she decided that she liked Matthew's, the reddish brown hugging the lines of his face, the eyes above warm and teasing. Her fingers curled against nothing, an unconscious expression of her desire to explore this man with touch.

His voice was clear and warm, gently teasing. 'I thought you would be running, after yesterday.'

She pushed her hands into her jacket pockets. She was tall enough that with him sitting, she could look down with the slight disdain that would have infuriated Tyler into a temper tantrum.

'Running? What are you talking about?' She realised that her words were not convincing.

'You.' He was smiling slightly with only his eyes, the deep tones of his voice penetrating. 'You're afraid to get too close to anyone. In Security Cove you ran after we made love. I think that yesterday, on that hill, you told me enough about yourself that you're wishing now you hadn't. So I figured that you'd be out here with the dawn, getting ready to run away again.'

She bit her lip and he asked gently, 'Am I right, angel?'

'Yes.' She looked along the length of his boat. 'But your boat was going to give me a problem. I'd have to move it to get out, and you might wake up.' And she had not really wanted to go, despite the dangerous way he affected her.

'I would have woken,' he agreed easily. 'I'm used to being at public wharfs, and it isn't unusual for fishermen to move a boat in the night when they're trying to make space for their boats. I usually wake up right away. I like to be sure the thing gets done right, that my boat is tied properly. So you wouldn't have escaped, angel.'

'I was going to wait,' she admitted, realising her unacknowledged plan as she spoke. 'I thought you would go up the hill and start painting, and I was going to wait until then.'

He grinned, said, 'It wouldn't have worked. I was going to ask you and Shane to come with us. Have you had a morning cup of coffee yet? Would you like one?'

'I'd love one.' She was smiling, feeling a sudden warmth that had no explanation. He was only gone a moment, coming back with a steaming mug and setting it on the ledge behind him.

She was not going to fight him. That would be undignified, likely to bring out the emotional imbalance that his presence seemed to create in her. She climbed across to his boat silently, picked up the mug and sat across from him, sipping silently, looking in through his wheelhouse windows because it was easier than looking at him, feeling happy and nervous all at once.

'You've tidied up in your wheelhouse. What happened to the mess? The paints?'

He seemed unaware of his hand going to her hair, brushing the softness away from her face before he leaned back and she could breathe again. 'I can't sail with all that mess. It's put away. The paints all have a place, a cupboard in the wheelhouse. The wet canvases are in the aft cabin. I've got racks for them there.'

She twisted to look back at the closed door to the aft cabin. 'Can I look?' she asked, needing action.

'No!' She was startled at the loudness of his voice, stared at his face and surprised something that might have been nervousness, or self-consciousness.

'Don't you like people to see your work? You didn't mind in Security Cove.' She had come through the wheelhouse, seeing and feeling the force of his painting against her will. Then, later, she had woken from the dream, his touch on her flesh, his lips....

She shivered, the memory open in her eyes, and Matthew watching, knowing. 'I'd like to see, but——' She shrugged, trying for indifference. 'It doesn't matter.'

'I'd like you to see them.' He put his cup down, and for an endless second she thought he was going to touch her. 'Most of my paintings—the ones in the aft cabin—they're of the islands, your islands. I'd like you to tell me if you think I've captured... whatever that magic is that these islands have. I can't put it in words, but I've tried to paint it.' He pushed an uneasy hand through his hair, said abruptly, 'Another day I'll show them to you.'

She was a little bewildered, and he could not explain about the semi-nude portrait of an angel stored in the aft cabin. He said, 'Angel, let's not look at paintings now. There's one that—I'm just not ready to show anyone. That's why I said—I feel a bit defensive about it.' That was the understatement of the century, but she seemed to accept it.

They watched the pink of dawn changing to the colours of day, and in one of the quiet, easy moments they spent sitting in his cockpit, he said, 'Angel, I wish you would stay for a few days.'

'Why?' Her eyes were guarded now, watching him, her body suddenly rigid. She said swiftly, 'I'm not going to—I don't want to have an affair with you.' She saw the sparkle in his eyes, felt the warmth rising inside herself, and said hurriedly, 'I know that you—it's true that I'm attracted to you, and if you tried I——' She tossed her hair back, creating a wild, swirling disarray and wishing she did not feel this terrible compulsion to be honest with him. 'I would be in your bed again, if you tried, but—Matthew, I don't want to feel like that. I don't want to have an affair.'

Behind her, up the hillside, she could hear a truck on the road that was hidden in the trees. It would be the caretaker of the abandoned settlement, the only inhabitant.

'All right, angel.'

She put her cup down, eyeing him suspiciously as he seemed to avoid her gaze. 'What do you mean by that?'

She liked his closely trimmed beard, but right now she wished she could see more of his face, could read what he was thinking as he said mildly, 'Let's just enjoy ourselves. Have some picnics up the hill, go for walks. Shane said he was wanting to go on to Anthony Island. We could go there in a few days, then start sailing back up the island in time for you to get Shane off to school. Anne would enjoy the extra company, and so would I. How long do you have?'

'Ten days more.' He was too relaxed, too comfortable, and she was not sure if she trusted him. 'Shane flies to Victoria in ten days. I don't think—I think we should go on, Shane and I . . . Alone.'

'Do you?' He sipped his coffee, his long, calloused fingers holding the cup loosely. 'Your son's got a lot of talent, you know. I'd like to spend some time with him.'

What was he doing? Was he really interested in Shane? She said tightly, her voice openly suspicious, 'I asked Shane what you said about his sketches. He didn't say anything, just looked uncomfortable.'

Matthew laughed. 'I wouldn't expect him to tell you what I said. It wasn't all complimentary. He's got talent, but he's picked up some very bad habits. If he wants to do anything with it, he'll have to work hard.'

'Is that what you told him?'

'No.' He leaned towards her, the coffee in one hand and the other brushing her leg fleetingly. She felt the touch through her jeans and almost jerked away from him. 'He wanted to know if I thought he could get into the College of Art. I looked at his sketches, and I told him that if he sent that portfolio to the College, he hadn't a chance of getting in.'

'Oh.' She tried very hard not to show her disappointment. No wonder Shane had been silent. He would have been hurt.

'Nicole—angel, he can get pretty compliments from you, or from his art teacher up at the high school. Sure, he's good—for a kid.'

She stood up. She had been wrong, thinking that Matthew might help Shane. She avoided his eyes, said, 'He doesn't have to measure up to your standards. He's just a teenager. He——'

'I also told him that if he worked hard, got some decent instruction over the next three years, no one could keep him out of that College. But he's got a hell of a long way to go.'

She met his eyes. His were a little defensive. She said softly, 'And of course you told him that? That he had a long way to go?'

'Of course.' He raked his hand through his hair, but the effect was not nearly as dramatic now that Bobbie had cut the brown locks short.

She couldn't help smiling. 'He's been working on those sketches ever since we left Queen Charlotte. Mostly he's frowning over things. There was a deer that he had a terrible time with.'

He nodded, understanding. 'I don't wonder. He has no idea of anatomy, either animal or human. We could work on the deer, Shane and I—if you stayed.' He touched her hair, brushing it back, but drawing his hand away before it could find its way to her cheek. 'You know, angel, I can read your mind. You're wondering if I'm using Shane to keep you here.'

'Can you blame me? You said you wanted to have an affair with me and——'

'—and I'm glad if Shane gives you a reason to stay, because I'm afraid otherwise you'd run away before we've a chance to get to know each other properly.'

'Properly? What does that mean?'

He stood up and removed the cup from her numbed fingers. 'Who knows, angel? I'm not sure I do, but I want to find out. I don't want to walk away and never see you again.' She had to look away, but he could see the unsteadiness around her lips, the nervousness in the way her fingers moved, and he changed the subject to one easier for them to discuss. 'I also do want to work with Shane. I'd never thought of myself teaching until recently, but the last couple of years I've done some workshops, and I'm amazed at how rewarding it is to share some of what I've learned, especially with young people who are so open, so eager to learn.'

Her fingers stopped trembling and she found herself smiling. 'Even if you talk as bluntly to them as you did to Shane?'

'I wouldn't talk like that to anyone who didn't have talent. Shane needs to realise that his talent isn't a substitute for work. That's the route to becoming a second-rater, and he's capable of much more than that.'

She thought of the oppressive paintings that had hung in Mrs Bentham's home and asked, 'Do you ever paint still lifes?'

'Pretty arrangements of flowers? I did some at art school—did some of everything at art school.' He grinned. 'It's not exactly my style, angel. I like something with a bit more bite in it.'

'I'll bet you do.' He had painted the shore of Security Cove with beauty and sadness twisted together into something more powerful than she could have seen if she had not looked at it through his eyes. 'Matthew, how did you get to art school? Did you always know it was what you wanted to do?'

'No.' He sat beside her this time, his arm stretched out and almost touching her shoulder. 'I grew up knowing exactly what I was going to be. It was the only thing Sam Kealy's son could be.' He saw her frowning, said, 'Yes, I thought that might ring a bell. After all, with your husband in law in Vancouver, you were bound to hear about Dad.'

'Judge Kealy? You were supposed to go to law school?'

'I did go, then I worked as junior partner in Dad's firm. That was just before he was made a judge. You should have seen me, angel.' He was laughing, his fingers touching the beard. 'Suits and ties and briefcases and—don't laugh!'

'Mountain Man, I'm trying to imagine you in a suit.' The thought of him in sleekly tailored garments was disquieting.

He looked down at his well-worn jeans and said with some satisfaction, 'I've gone to a lot of trouble to get rid of that image. I'll confess to you that I do have a suit in my hanging locker. I wear it when occasion demands—usually for my parents, so Dad won't be too upset at the sight of me.'

He was smiling as if his rough life-style were a gentle joke between him and his father. 'What happened?' she asked. 'How did you get from suits and a briefcase to this?'

She saw the way he watched the sky, the free wildness that emerged in his paintings, and she had trouble believing that he could have been anything but imprisoned and unhappy as a city lawyer. 'How did you stand it?' she wondered.

'I hated it, but I was trying to keep the people I loved happy. Dad...my mother——' He grinned and gestured around him. 'The boat is named after my mother. My father bought it for all of us to go sailing when Bobbie and I were small. Mom's a bit of a wild thing, but she would do anything to please my father, including pretending that sailing didn't frighten her.' He shrugged and said, 'There was more than that. My whole life manoeuvring me into position. After law school I began to feel I was being smothered. Until then I'd had time, energy to get away, go sketching and painting—it was just a release for me, a way to get rid of the tensions.'

The silence stretched. Soon Anne and Shane would wake, and these private moments would be gone. Nicole wanted to stretch them, to turn this interlude into an eternity, treasuring the closeness, the feeling of warmth without any demands.

Finally she asked, 'What happened after law school?'

'I did all the things I was supposed to.' His face was shadowed with the echo of the tension from that past. 'I was winning cases for clients, but half the time my mind was elsewhere, and the tension was building without my knowing. There was a girl, too, and everyone had always assumed we would marry. With me established, and her finished at university, it seemed like the right time—the logical time.'

'You got married?' She remembered her sadness when she had believed Bobbie was his wife. 'What was her name?'

'Gail. We were engaged, not married, hadn't actually set the date for the wedding.' And they were lovers. She knew that from his voice. 'Then Bobbie came home for a week. She dragged me away for a weekend on *Charmaine*, and told me I was destroying myself, that I was getting hard and brittle and unhappy.' He laughed, and she could hear his affection for his sister. 'The little brat! She tore me apart, then she went away and left me alone on the boat, and I had a hell of a lot of thinking to do.'

Overhead, two eagles circled, playing or preparing to fight. It was hard to tell which. Matthew said, 'I wasn't ready to go back when the weekend was over. I phoned Dad, hoped he would understand even though I didn't. It took me a week to realise how out of touch with myself I'd become, and another week to come to terms with disappointing everyone I cared about.'

He shrugged, although his voice told her that it had not been an easy decision, then he smiled and said, 'It was a kid about Shane's age that started making everything seem clear. There I was, playing hookey and not really sure what to do with myself. I had found an old sketch-pad and some charcoals aboard *Charmaine*, and

I was on the beach drawing people and waves, enjoying myself as if I were in some kind of illicit heaven. I used to do a lot of drawing. It always made me feel good, gave me new life, but somehow the legal business had taken over everything. It had been a couple of years since I'd touched a charcoal.'

He had the look in his eyes that always reminded her of flying high over everything, the feeling she had when the plane and the clouds and the blue infinity were all part of her.

Matthew said, 'This kid came up and started watching me. At first it distracted me, then I forgot about him. I was sketching an old man who was walking on the beach, trying to get his profile right on the paper.

'When I gave up, I'd got it as close as I could. I'd forgotten the boy, but when I started putting things away, he was there. When he asked, "You're an artist, aren't you?" I found myself saying "Yes," and somehow everything seemed simple.

'I didn't want to hurt Gail, or my father, but if I didn't get out of law soon, I never would. I had no idea if I could make a go of painting, though I knew I had a lot to learn before I could even try. I had to go to art school.' He shrugged away the details, two days of figuring out money and practicalities. 'I went back and told everyone.'

It would have been hard. She had never been able to tell her own father that she could not fulfil his dream. He had only wanted her to be happy, and she had hidden the unhappiness of her marriage from him until he died.

Matthew said, 'I didn't deserve it, but they all understood. Dad signed *Charmaine* over to Bobbie and I, and Bobbie said she would take her share in sailing trips. The boat became my home, and a very economical one. Without that I would have had trouble getting through art school on my savings, but I lived on the public wharfs at Vancouver, and when I graduated I had enough money left to sail away and give myself a year of semi-starvation and painting instead of looking for work in advertising.' He grinned, said, 'My grandmother left me most of that money, and I'm sure she never intended me to use it for anything as frivolous as art school.'

She found herself touching the crease of his forehead where the frown showed. He said, 'I felt worst about Gail, but she was not the kind of girl to dedicate herself to years of poverty in exchange for a faint chance of my making a living for her. I didn't ask her to do that, and I'm sure she was glad that I didn't. She married my cousin a year later, and as far as I can tell they've been happy enough. Happier than she would have been with me, because I could have married her and spent another five years making us both miserable and discovering I couldn't live that way.'

There must have been other women after Gail. In his arms she had felt like the only woman in the universe, but it was foolish to think that there had not been many others. He was the rolling stone, gathering no moss, meeting and touching and sailing away with the dawn when he grew restless.

Yet, here at Tasu, he seemed content to stay for ever. The days stretched into a week while Nicole tried to tell herself she should go while she could still escape with her heart intact.

Matthew and Shane took sketch-pads up into the hills, and Shane learned about animals, about muscles and bones and the way deer moved when they ran.

They took Matthew's dinghy and motored all around Tasu Sound, finding a road on the far side and walking miles inland, Anne riding first on Matthew's shoulders and then on Shane's. They came to a beautiful clearing, where moss grew in a soft carpet, and they all fell on to the soft ground, exhausted, and ate the lunch they had prepared.

Anne and Shane were ready to move again first, and they went off looking for a stream to use for cool drinking water. Matthew and Nicole were left alone.

He was lying flat on his back, his hands behind his head, staring up at patterns of clouds on brilliant blue. She was sitting nearby, leaning up against a tree trunk that had been placed by nature just for her. The tree must have been hundreds of years old, part of the ancient forest of the south island.

Nicole was watching Matthew while pretending to watch the path where Shane and Anne had disappeared. Seven perfect days. She was trying not to count, but it felt as if Tasu were turning into for ever, even while she knew how hard leaving was going to be.

'Tomorrow we have to leave.'

She had not meant to say the words, but they were echoing through the clearing. She bit her lip and watched Matthew, but he did not move, did not turn to look at her. He was watching the clouds. He looked terribly serious.

He said, 'We seem to have a problem, angel.'

'Do we?' Her voice was brittle. Tomorrow. She and Shane would leave. She would miss Matthew terribly, but it would be over. The problem would be the leaving, not afterwards, because it would be done then, and there would be no going back.

'Yes.' His elbow moved, pointing to her, and his head turned so that he could look across the few feet that separated them. 'Angel, I still want to have an affair with you.'

Her heart was pounding, drowning out the sound of the bumblebee who was exploring the other side of the old tree where she sat. She felt her tongue slipping out to touch her lips, to impart moisture where sudden dryness had grown.

He said, 'But you don't believe in casual affairs. Is that right?'

'Yes.' Her voice was so faint that he probably could not hear, but she said the word, agreeing with him, ignoring the powerful urge to deny it, to stand up and stumble across the clearing, throwing herself into his arms again.

She saw his eyes narrow. 'There's only one solution then, isn't there, angel?'

'Yes,' she agreed, grasping at the words. 'We have to say goodbye. Tomorrow.'

Tomorrow was only one sleep away. If it were not for Shane and Anne, unwitting chaperons, she knew that she would leave her bed tonight and climb across the boats in the dark, going to him. Once more. Just once.

Matthew said, 'I really can't do that,' and she felt the terrible oppression from the heat of the sun. She stumbled to her feet and went to the huckleberry bush to fumble with the small, dark berries.

'What are you talking about?' Her voice was muffled. She was not sure any more if she could say no to the affair he wanted.

She would have to go home, then Shane would get on the jet to go away to school. If Matthew came then, wanting her, she did not think she could refuse him.

When his words came, they hit her with the shock of freezing water. 'We'll have to get married.'

She backed two more steps, stumbling over the bush, panic in her eyes and in the tension of her body.

'No! No, Matthew! I couldn't—I couldn't do that again. I—I really could not bear it. You—you couldn't either. You don't want that, ties and—no!'

He nodded, and she had a feeling that he had known how she would react. 'Then it will have to be my way, won't it, angel? Either that, or I'll follow you around these islands until you give in.'

She gulped. 'You mean, and have an affair with you?'

'That's what I mean.' There was a long moment of silence, then he said, 'You could make up your mind now. When your son goes, you could take a couple of weeks more, come with me aboard *Charmaine*.'

She thought she might be on the verge of an asthma attack, although she had never been susceptible to asthma before. 'You—you mean, if I go with you, you—two weeks, and then you'll—leave me alone.' He nodded and she swallowed, said, 'Are you sure?'

'It's a promise, angel.'

She pushed her hair back. At first she thought it was starting to rain, the wet dampening her soft cloud of hair. Then she realised that it was her, the moisture from a cold sweat that must be panic or terror. 'That sounds horrible. Two weeks, a cold affair.'

'Not cold. I can promise you that. And I think you know it would be anything but casual. And if you don't want an affair, there's always the other alternative.'

'The other...'

'Marrying me.' He sounded grim, and he said, 'Figure out what your price is. If it's marriage, then I'll pay it.'

'Why?' He didn't answer, and she felt herself spinning, the past and present mixing. 'You'll marry me? Have you thought about that? What do you plan? To move to Queen Charlotte? To live on my boat? Your boat? A house?' He shrugged, his eyes watchful, and she had a horrible conviction that he could see the insanity inside her that almost had her grabbing, saying yes to something that never could work.

When he would say nothing, she said bitterly, 'Marriage would be easy for you, wouldn't it? A licence, a service, and then the affair you say you want. Then you would go, disappear. I—I don't know why you think you want me. There are other women and——'

'None like you.' He was frowning, and she was almost sure his voice held resentment. 'None that have me obsessed like you do.'

'Then paint me!' She felt her trembling mouth with her fingers, looked down and picked a fat blue berry, put it into her mouth and swallowed. 'That's how you get rid of your obsessions, isn't it?'

'I tried. The painting only makes it worse.' Holding his eyes hurt something deep inside her. She looked away, at the hard lines of him, his thighs, his broad chest. He said, 'I need to have you, angel.'

She gasped, 'God! That's all I need! Another man forced to marry me for a roll in the hay.' Only, Tyler had got her pregnant first. 'At least you're not lying to me, telling me you love me.' She was going to cry, and she would not let him see. She ground out, 'Damn it, Matthew! I've asked you to leave me alone! Will you please go away? Please!'

CHAPTER NINE

SHE woke to the music pounding in her ears. The clouds had darkened the early morning, and the oppressive grey outside her porthole was at one with the orchestra pounding, pressing down on her.

She felt heavy, hardly able to move. It was like the days of Mrs Bentham, the time before she had discovered the Queen Charlottes and *Island Wanderer*, before she had realised that escape was possible for her and Shane.

She was trembling, eyes closed tightly, her spirit shrivelling and crying.

Nicole, don't talk to that woman. She's not our kind.

Nicole, not that dress!

My goodness, Nicole! How could you have bought those clothes for Shane? Why, he looks like the gardener's son!

Nicole, you aren't going flying again, are you? I was talking to Heather Steinworth the other day, and she said that it's really a bit odd, your spending so much time flying.

The flying club was her only escape. Otherwise there was the voice of the woman she could not bear to call mother. And the music, that endless, horrible music waking her each morning, the oppression growing and the volume increasing with each week. Nicole hid everything inside, never letting anyone see, but it was there. That sick dread, the feeling that made her understand the caged monkeys at Stanley Park.

The headache grew with the sounds, pain pulsing with every thrust of a violin string, with each pounding surge of violence. When she could stand it no longer she found herself standing, bare feet on the varnished wooden floor.

But it would not stop. The pounding, the horrible, endless pain surging behind her eyes. She pulled her robe around her and staggered out, past the open door to the cabin where Shane slept, up the steps and into the cockpit.

He was there, painting, and the sound was everywhere, all around him, echoing off the mountains and the low, grey sky. She tried to speak, to tell him to turn it off, but the words were all tied up, somehow held in by the violence in the air.

She stumbled past him, into his wheelhouse, not knowing whether he saw her or spoke to her. Not caring. Nothing mattered except the horrible, pounding headache. She searched frantically with eyes aching with the pain.

Nothing.

The speakers, there in each corner of the windscreen. But where was it coming from? Where?

Some part of her heard or sensed motion behind her, but she pushed it away, moving to the console built into the wall near the inside steering wheel. Lights surging across in a pulse from green to red, keeping time with the pain behind her eyes.

She pushed a button and the silence flooded in, filling the void. Her head was ringing, not ready to accept the absence of the music. She pushed the button marked *eject* and it was in her hand, a small plastic cassette that trapped those sounds.

His hands went to her shoulders as she turned and she screamed, 'Let go of me! Let me go!' and she was past him, out in his cockpit, her arm pulled back and thrusting in one violent throw that sent the small black cassette flying over the water.

She watched it until the rings on the water dispersed to nothing. When it was gone, the tension flowed out of her and she felt limp and exhausted.

Behind her, Matthew asked wryly, 'Do you feel that way about all Dvořák's music, or just that piece?'

She turned, and he was there, so close behind her that she should have felt his presence as she watched the cassette tape dropping into the water. The violence had left her and she felt embarrassed and ashamed of herself, but she did not know what words she could say.

He was watching her the way he had watched the deer on the hill the other day, and she saw his fingers move as if they wished they held a brush or a charcoal. He said slowly, 'You know, it's always a shock when the emotions inside you come boiling out. You're so cool, so controlled. I know it's only a facade, because I can see your eyes, but sometimes it seems that your control is so total, the emotions will never break free.'

She could not talk, so he went on. 'The night I made love to you, you were another woman, the woman I see when I look in your eyes. The woman who just tore my favourite cassette out of my stereo and threw it into the ocean.'

'I hate that music. I can't—Mrs Bentham... *every* morning I woke up to it. When I hear it I think I'm back in that house, with that woman, trapped and...' She felt the emotion ringing in the air. 'Matthew, I don't—that's not how I usually am. I don't know what's been getting into me lately. I've got to get myself under control. I'm sorry.'

'I'm not.' She felt his touch on her cheek, although his hands did not move. 'I don't think you should be sorry, either. It's time you learned to come to terms with your own emotions.' She shook her head, but he ignored her denial. 'Did you always call her Mrs Bentham?'

'No.' Her hands found her hair a wild chaos. Had she been running, tossing her hair back, her motions as wild as the feelings boiling inside? 'I usually managed to avoid calling her by any name. I was supposed to call her *Mother*.'

He nodded, and she believed that he had seen everything about the relationship between Nicole and her mother-in-law. 'She has to control everything.' The words were saying themselves, without her permission. 'I'm constantly afraid that she'll get hold of Shane. Tyler left everything to Shane, with her as trustee. I haven't touched any of it, and I've tried to keep Shane away from it. If she controls his finances, she'll try to control him, too. That terrifies me, that I'll lose him to her.'

'You won't.' He took her shoulders in his hands, his thumbs gently massaging the tension away. 'He loves you. But, angel, you're going to lose him to the world. He's growing up. He'll always love you, but he can't be your world any longer.'

'He isn't,' she denied, her face flushing from the truth in his words. 'I've got my job, and——'

'And what else? Who else?' He brushed her lips with his and her mouth opened to him, an invitation she could not have held back if she had wanted to. He took her kiss gently, a muted passion that glowed along her veins as his voice murmured, 'Angel, you're the most beautiful woman.'

His arms felt the curves through her thin robe, his broad chest accepting the thrust of her breasts, his tongue exploring the warm darkness of her mouth. The world was spinning, bright despite the greyness overhead. She felt a shuddering wave of surrender go throughout her body and her heart, and her arms were sliding up, around his neck, her fingers glorying in the sensations of hair and skin.

'Beautiful,' he growled as his teeth tenderly possessed her lower lip.

'No.' Her head tipped back in denial, exposing the soft, defenceless flesh of her neck to his lips. She felt the trembling growing as his hands moulded her hips against him, his lips moving down her neck, a warm tongue slipping out against the sensitive beginnings of fullness that were exposed by the V of her robe at the neck. 'No,' she moaned, wishing his kisses were silent, unable to bear anything that could be even the shadow of a lie. 'Not beautiful. You know I'm not beautiful.'

His hands slid all along her back, gliding on the sleek, soft fabric of her robe. Across her shoulders, down the ridges of muscle and flesh along both sides of her spine, to the sensitive hollows at the base of her spine. Down, further, possessing the roundness of her buttocks and draining her legs of strength.

She was weak, helpless, sagging against him, his willing arms holding her, his lips caressing, his short beard sending an erotic surge of tingling pleasure through her as he pushed aside her robe with his chin.

One moment of clear self-knowledge penetrated the erotic haze, the trembling pleasures of his lips on her breast.

She wanted him, needed him with an aching that could not be denied. In a second his mouth would find the erect nipple that his lips were probing for, and she would groan aloud because nothing could hold back the response of her flesh and her heart to this man.

Then he would take her hand and lead her forward, to the cabin in the bow of his boat, where the door would close, and lock. She prayed that Anne and Shane would sleep on through the early morning.

She needed him.

She pushed the word *love* away. She could never love again. It's sex, she told herself desperately, and reached for the drugging pleasure of his lips against her heated body, felt her fingers trembling against him. A physical attraction...need...obsession, and tomorrow was forever away. Only this day, this moment, this shuddering instant in time existed.

She wanted to cry at him not to speak, to silence the words, but his lips were moving away from her breast and she was pressing herself hard against him, her body crying for his nearness.

'Soon,' he whispered, his hand taking her fingers and threading them through his, drawing her across the cockpit. He bent down to her and his lips possessed hers in a hard, searing kiss that drew a passionate response from her. She was kissing him back, her tongue entangled with his, the darkness of two mouths twined together. Then he drew back, his husky voice insisting, 'Beautiful angel. Come with me. Let me show you.'

'I want you.' A whisper, not Nicole's voice but a husky, heated woman open to her man.

'You know how I want you, too,' he groaned, his lips clinging to hers again briefly before he pulled her with him, opened the door to the after cabin. 'First, you have to see. Come, see how beautiful you are.'

The open doorway was solid, a foundation for her to sag against. He let the teak door-frame support her while she reached out and linked her hands behind his head, whispering seductively, 'Matthew, kiss me... please...touch me...kiss me...everywhere.'

His lips explored the soft, trembling lids that covered her eyes, the curve of her cheek. His hands shaped the free roundness of her breasts under the robe, his thumbs rubbing across the rigid arousal of her nipples.

'Open your eyes,' he instructed her. Her lids uncovered blue eyes, deepened almost to black. 'I painted you like that,' he whispered hoarsely. 'Look.' He drew her against him, turning her towards the doorway. 'Look, and tell me that you are not the most beautiful woman.' His fingers trembled against her back and he whispered, 'Portrait of an angel.'

There was stillness, everywhere, and a silence that screamed to the hills and the sky. His arms were holding her, but it was the painting that touched her, surrounded her.

She was lying tangled in the covers, half covered, yet obviously naked beneath the twisted quilt. Her face was soft, the lips parted. Her eyes...

She swallowed, feeling what that woman felt. It was her, Nicole Bentham, lying naked and vulnerable in the aftermath of arousal, her eyes telling the man who watched that she was his, that her mysteries were revealed to him alone.

Yet it was more than a portrait, because he had seen within, too far for comfort, and her painted eyes told her things that she had kept secret even from herself.

'No,' she whispered, the coldness surging up in waves. She pulled back, and his arm fell away from her when he saw her face. 'No! You had no right! You——' Her eyes closed on a painful spasm, then she jerked towards the painting, reaching out, needing to conceal, to destroy that vision of herself.

He caught her, hard. 'No!'

She would not meet his eyes. His arms imprisoned her and she could not pull away. She said with a tight, hard anger, 'I won't be painted as some cheap nude.'

'It's not a nude.'

It wasn't. In the painting, the woman's body was covered, although anyone looking would know that there were no clothes under that quilt. She could not look away, and finally she realised that it was the eyes that were so nakedly exposed.

'Take your arm away from me.' She sounded like her mother-in-law, her voice cold and hard and that of a woman who had never loved, would never love.

He was silent, but watching her as if he owned what he saw. The way he looked at the deer, the hills. Her lungs hurt when she tried to breathe, but the words came.

'If you ever paint me again, I—if that painting ever——' Speech seemed to suck away her control. In seconds, she would be screaming, and then she might say anything, do anything. And he would see, his eyes looking past the woman that was Nicole Bentham, past her barriers that no one was supposed to be able to penetrate.

She took several ragged breaths, then managed a cold voice. 'I'll sue you,' she said tightly. She backed away from him as if he were pursuing. 'Get rid of that painting, or I'll sue you.'

Then she was running, stumbling over his lifelines and on to her own deck, then on to the old float they were tied to. She slipped as she half ran towards the ramp, then she was on the gravel, on solid ground, and walking fast, escaping to where the trees might make it seem as if Matthew Kealy and *Charmaine* did not exist.

If there was any place that far away.

She slowed when she had crossed the abandoned causeway that led from the old town to the mine site. He had not caught up with her, was not pursuing her.

He would not follow. She was not sure what she was running from, because she had seen his eyes just before she turned and fled.

He had never looked at her like that before, but she would not be surprised if he was gone by the time she came back down the hill.

There was no way that he would destroy that painting.

He did not watch her go. She was fleeing him, and if he pursued he would only find the cold, controlled Nicole. Not the woman he loved.

Damn! He had not asked for her, had not wanted to love her. For weeks now he had been telling himself that it was compulsion, obsession, that the painting would free him of her. If not the painting, then only one thing would free him. Holding her in his arms, possessing her again.

An affair. Brief and hot and all-consuming. For the world, she had the coolness of a chaste, blonde angel. When he touched her, sometimes her eyes changed, and her mouth softened to invitation and need. Then she was his woman.

If it could have remained an obsession, he would be free now. He had the painting, and for one glorious night he had possessed the woman. Then, again, for brief moments, she had been his this morning. They had not consummated their mutual need before she ran, but she had been as much his this morning as she had been that first night.

More, because now he knew her. He knew her mind, the soft laughter that he could sometimes bring to her lips, the quiet love she had for her son, her warmth for his small niece. He knew the look in her eyes when she was thinking of flying, soaring in the sky like a bird.

And that other look—the soft, frightened look that told him she was afraid of her emotions, her feelings. He had brought that look to her eyes, often. He had hoped, here in the almost completely abandoned wilderness town of Tasu, to soothe the fears, to hold out his arms and see her come to him with her eyes warm and open and willing.

Then they could have loved together for a short while before they went on their separate ways. What it amounted to, he admitted as he stared at the painting, was that he wanted her to love him for a while. However, Tyler Bentham, damn him, had hurt her badly enough that she was never going to love any man again. Why else had she lived alone except for Shane ever since she came to these islands?

There was no reason for staying, not now.

He put away the canvas in the wheelhouse, hanging it securely on one of the racks he had built to hold wet oils secure during sailing. The easel folded and locked into its place under the port deck.

As he collected tubes of oil paint that seemed to have scattered everywhere, he heard Anne mumbling in her sleep. His niece was sleeping on the wide settee on the port side of the salon. The same settee where he and Nicole...

He put on a kettle to boil. Soon he would wake Anne, if she did not come stumbling out herself, rubbing her eyes and asking for the hot chocolate that was a morning ritual.

Once she'd had her chocolate, and a bowl of cereal, he would untie the lines and *Charmaine* would part company from *Island Wanderer*. Anne would be unhappy to leave Shane, and Matthew would be unhappy too, but perhaps he should have done it long ago.

He looked out and saw Shane standing at the door of the aft cabin, staring in at the painting of his mother. Matt stepped through the open door and stood behind Shane, but he didn't know what to say to the boy. He could see Nicole's image in oils over Shane's shoulder, was thankful that the most intimate curves of his angel's flesh had not been exposed to his brush. When Shane turned to look at him, the boy's eyes were a cross between resentment and curiosity.

Matt said simply, 'I love her.'

The boy swallowed, looking back at the painting. 'Are you—will you sell that one?'

'No.' Matt knew it was good, because just looking at it made him ache to take her in his arms, to touch that glorious gold cloud of soft hair, to tell her not to be frightened, that they had all the time in the world. He said to Shane, 'I painted it for me. To look at when I'm gone from here.'

It was not true that they had time. They had nothing more, only his memories and what his brush and his heart had put on the canvas.

Shane pushed his hands into his pockets, trying to look nonchalant. 'You're leaving now, aren't you?'

'Yes.' He reached past the boy and closed the door to the aft cabin. It had been a mistake to show her the painting, but there was no point now in staying. The portrait had told her how he felt, and she did not want to hear, had run in terror.

'I guess I'll never see you again.' Shane's eyes were downcast, watching the toe of his shoe dig at the cockpit floor. 'I'm goin' to Victoria in a few days.'

Matt realised then that the boy was hurt. He dropped a hand on his shoulder and said, 'I don't see why not. You'll be at St Michael's school, won't you? I'm going down south in November for a showing of my paintings in Vancouver. I'll pop over to Victoria and take you out for a day. You can show me what you've been doing, and we'll go out for dinner somewhere.'

'McDonalds?' suggested Shane.

'Sure,' agreed Matt, 'Anywhere you want. I'll drop you a letter the beginning of November to give you the date. And here——' He leaned in and took a card from the ledge over the chart table. 'That's my address if you want to write. It takes a while for my mail to catch up to me, so don't be surprised if it takes me a few weeks to answer.'

Shane took the card and pushed it into his jeans pocket. 'I'll write to you. And Mom says I can take extra art lessons when I'm at school in Victoria. Matt, you and Mom—you had a fight, didn't you? I heard her shouting at you, and she never shouts. Are you going to go without seein' her again? What—what if she wants to make up?'

Matt shook his head. 'No, son. She's not going to want to make up. Sometimes—don't worry about it, Shane. There's no reason you and I can't still be friends.'

But not Nicole.

After Anne had had her breakfast, Shane helped Matt untie the boat and he left. *Charmaine* crossed Tasu Sound and cleared the narrow entrance to the sea. By noon, they were out of sight of land, heading south, away from both *Island Wanderer* and Queen Charlotte City.

He wished he had never shown her the picture. If he hadn't, he could have stayed, and she would not have run. They could have been friends, if not lovers. His mind sheered away from the other possibility.

Marriage. He had been badly ridden by his obsession when he made that offer. He had known it was safe, that she would reject it, that she was too wary of marriage after Tyler. Yet, when she had refused almost without stopping to think, he had felt sharp disappointment, as if a warm vision of the future had dissolved into barren nothingness.

He was an artist, and obviously he had a hell of a lot more artistic temperament than he'd thought. Romantic. Unrealistic. What did he want? She was right. A marriage would never work between a careful pilot and a wandering artist, and there was no way he could settle down, stay in one place. He hadn't been willing to do it for Gail, and nothing had changed.

Or had it?

No, damn it! He would not go back, would not beg her to marry him. It wouldn't make any difference anyway. She didn't want him on any terms—no, that was wrong. She *wanted* him, but only in moments of passion. And, damn it, she would love him too, if only she would let herself. But she didn't want love, and he could not fight that. Whenever she stopped to think, she started running.

He would be crazy to try to capture a woman like that.

CHAPTER TEN

WITH Shane gone away to school, the loneliness became almost unbearable.

The evenings were the worst, and the weekends. The boat seemed empty, hollow. She tried to tell herself that it was nice to have the time and the peace to do all the little jobs she had been wanting to attend to. Clearing out the hatches under Shane's bunk. Organising the food stores into logical order. Getting out her sewing machine and making a new cover for the mainsail.

She did all of those jobs, and others that did not need doing, but, when everything was tidy and shipshape and clean, the boat was still empty. For weeks she pretended that it was only Shane's absence creating the empty ache in her heart. Her son was gone to school, and, although he would come back for summers and holidays, it would never be quite the same again. He was growing up, growing away, and she had not expected the emptiness.

She signed up for a night-school class in painting. She knew little about art, had no particular talent, and trying to learn made her ache for both Shane and Matthew, but the classes helped to pass the time.

Thank God for her work! If she could not fly, she thought that she would go insane. She accepted every flight Luke offered, and September was a busy month, but with October came the slow time, and winter would be worse.

Shane wrote every week, and she was relieved to read happiness between the lines of his letter. She had been a little worried, sending this northern island child out to a big city boarding-school, but Shane seemed excited about new friends and endless activities.

He had grown out of his shoes and trousers and needed almost all new clothes. He needed money for the mountain-climbing club too, and for art supplies. He was taking art classes twice a week and his instructor said that he had talent. Nicole sent him money for the clothes, the mountain-climbing club, and the art supplies. It was a good thing that she had a lot of flying hours in and hardly any expenses of her own.

In one letter, Shane said, 'Matt is coming to visit me in November. He's going to look at my sketches and take me out for a day. I'm trying to get as good at sketching as I can before he comes. He's going to treat me to dinner at McDonalds.'

Nicole cried that night, and she knew that the tears were not for Shane. She missed her son terribly, but he was healthy and happy and she would see him at Christmas and summer, but she might never see Matthew Kealy again...

He had left Tasu, and she had not known where he might have gone, except that there was no sign of *Charmaine*, and Shane had said he was gone and behaved as if it were her fault.

She and Shane had returned home, leaving the same day Matthew did, and not seeing any sign of him. After Shane left, Nicole found herself searching the water below her plane every time she flew. One day, flying the lighthouse keeper's wife back to Cape St James on the southern extreme of the islands, she saw a big white sail flying over teak decks. She circled down, her heart pounding and her breath gone, but the hull of the boat was dark green, not blue, and there were four people on board who waved enthusiastically at the seaplane.

The lighthouse keeper's wife was wearing her spare set of headphones, and she said, 'Pretty boat,' her voice coming over the intercom to Nicole's ears.

What would she have done if the boat had been his? Taken this woman home, then come back and searched for *Charmaine*? What would she say to him?

She should have been watching the horizon, the blue water and the hills, but the picture in front of her eyes was the picture Matthew had painted of her, and the plane jerked and trembled, and it was Nicole's hands that made the flight rough, although her passenger said good-naturedly, 'Lots of turbulence in the air today.'

It wasn't the air, it was the pilot, and she made sure that she did not let it happen again.

After the lighthouse, she had a mail drop in Tasu, then the flight home to Queen Charlotte. She tied up her plane and spent a while talking to Barry in the office, then went into the coffee room and sat reading a magazine and drinking coffee, not wanting to go home to the boat, half hoping for another call and a flight to keep her busy into the evening hours.

Luke came in and poured himself a cup of coffee.

'The coffee's pretty old,' she told him. 'Terribly strong.' She should not be drinking it, because the last thing she needed was another sleepless night.

Luke drank it anyway. He liked his coffee strong and black, and he never seemed to care when it had been made. 'I had a charter to Rose Harbour,' he told her.

'Oh? Who? The people who live down there?' Rose Harbour was on the southern part of the south islands. Once it had been a whaling station, but now it was privately owned.

'No. Matthew Kealy and his niece. I flew them into Sandspit to catch the jet to Vancouver.'

She could not even pretend that it did not matter, because he was watching, and he seemed to know. Mercifully, he did not make her ask for more information, but told her, 'He's leaving his boat moored at Rose Harbour. He's taking his niece down to her mother and staying a couple of weeks, then he'll be flying back and taking the boat directly south to Vancouver Island.'

'Did—Luke, did he ask about me?' She felt herself flushing under his questioning gaze, then paling as he shook his head.

'No, Nick. Sorry.'

She shook her head and said, 'It's all right.'

But it wasn't. She told herself that it would be easier now that he was gone, and in a way it was. She stopped watching for his boat when she came down to the docks each evening. She stopped looking for his boat on the water under her when she flew. One day she diverted a flight and circled down over the boat moored in Rose Harbour.

Even though *Charmaine* was abandoned, her owner in Vancouver, she felt an ache in her throat when she recognised the blue hull and the wooden mast. She almost landed and went aboard, but she knew that he was not there, and the people who lived on shore might think she was a prowler or a thief, although surely it was unusual for boats to be robbed or vandalised by people who flew down from out of the sky.

Sometimes she dreamed that she would get the flight when he came back, that Barry would call her ten minutes before she landed at the base and say, 'Pick-up for you here when you get back. Customer wants to fly to Rose Harbour.'

In those dreams, she flew with the man she loved at her side, and tried to tell him she loved him. Sometimes he touched her gently, his eyes seeing what he had when he'd painted her. Once, in a dream, he asked her to land, somewhere there were no other people. She circled and set down in a deserted inlet, and he took her into his arms and told her that he had been aching for her ever since he sailed away at Tasu. In the dream, she was not sure where the inlet was, but later—awake—she thought that it must have been Rockfish Harbour.

But when she woke up she was always alone, her mouth dry and frightened because she wanted to see him, and she was terrified that if she saw him she would not be able to find the courage to tell him——

Tell him what? Would he want to hear that she loved him? He had never talked about love, and that one mention of marriage had been an offer he'd known she would not accept.

Once, he had wanted an affair with her. She should have had the sense to tell him yes, to reach out and have whatever she could of this man. It would have been wonderful, glorious, like reaching for the heavens and finding them in your grasp.

If she had walked into his arms when he'd asked, trusting him . . . trusting . . .

No, this was not Tyler. Her husband had seduced her into his bed by telling her that he loved her, wanted her as his wife one day when he was established in his profession, that love was for ever and loving meant giving.

She had loved and given everything she had, and when the precautions failed and she became pregnant Tyler had consented to marry her, yet now she believed that he had never believed in his own words when he'd promised to forsake all others.

Matthew had not made any promises, no declarations of love. If she walked into his arms, if he still wanted her, it might not last for ever. Perhaps only a few days, or weeks, but they would be the best days, and perhaps afterwards they could still be friends.

She would not ask for anything he could not give, and he would not lie to her. She trusted him. It had terrified her when she had seen that painting he had done, because he seemed to have seen right through to her soul, but she was getting used to the idea of the painting. It was scary, knowing he could see through all her barriers, but he was the one person in the world that she believed she could trust. He might not love her, but what he felt was more than liking, and he would never knowingly hurt her.

I love you, Matthew.

She said it out loud one day when she was flying high over the water, alone. The words echoed around her, and it felt good, saying them.

If it was at all possible, she wanted to be the one to fly him back to his boat. Of course she would not tell him that she loved him. He might not want to hear that. It was like asking for things he could not give, for marriage and commitment. If he gave her anything, it must be freely given, not a trap like the one she had unwittingly shared with Tyler.

She would tell him that she was sorry she had got so angry, that she had not meant what she said about the painting. She would ask him if he would please not let anyone else see it, though. She thought he would understand that, and agree. If he had plans to sell the painting, perhaps he would let her buy it.

She didn't know what his paintings cost, but she would find the money somehow, and she would hang the portrait on the wall at the end of her bunk, a reminder that he had once seen her as a beautiful angel.

She hoped he would not want to sell, because that would mean he wanted the painting for himself. It was not very likely, and she was crying when she thought about it. A good thing that there were no passengers in the plane to see the pilot sobbing, tears running down her cheeks.

When she landed in Queen Charlotte, Luke was at the seaplane dock and helped her tie up. When he asked her what was wrong, she grimaced and simply said, 'I'm just realising what a fool I was.'

He did not ask what she meant, and she had a crazy feeling that he understood.

She piloted the scheduled flight to Prince Rupert the next day, and managed to get stranded for three days by fog that lay over Rupert Harbour and would not lift. By the time she returned to Queen Charlotte City, Matthew was gone.

'I flew him to Rose Harbour two days ago,' Luke told her. He was in a hurry, loading up for a rush flight to the west coast, and he sounded unusually impatient as he said, 'Look, Nick, I want to get out of here and get this charter done. Laurie and I want to get away together this weekend. We're going to go camping for a couple of days while the weather's still decent. Could you take the Cessna and go down to Hotspring Island? You'll have to stay overnight, because there's a bunch of stuff to be ferried from Hotspring over to Lyell Island.'

Matthew was gone. Would he still be on the islands? Or would he have already crossed to the mainland?

'You'll take this flight, won't you?' Luke sounded irritated, in a hurry to be gone himself. 'Take the Cessna. It's got amphibious floats. Be sure you've got a sleeping-bag. You can sleep in the cabin on Hotspring Island.'

She would fly to Rose Harbour first. If she was lucky, Matthew might still be there. Maybe he was waiting there for good weather to make the long crossing. The patchy fog might have kept him on the islands.

Please, God. Let him be there still.

She flew directly to Rose Harbour, ignoring the twinge of guilt as she passed Hotspring Island. This flight had seemed to have some urgency, and she should have asked Luke if it was all right to take half an hour for a side trip of her own before landing at Hotspring.

She circled over Rose Harbour twice, trying not to believe her own eyes, but there was no doubt. Three boats were tied to the moorings at Rose Harbour, but none of them were sail-boats. He was gone.

She could fly out looking for him, but he would be a day ahead of her, or two days. She had searched for missing boats, missing aircraft, and knew that one small boat on the open ocean could elude searchers for weeks... for ever.

She was circling over Hotspring Island before she realised that Luke had not told her the name of the customer. She was a little surprised to find that there was no boat anchored in front of the island. She circled twice and finally decided there must be a dinghy somewhere, pulled up on shore out of her sight, and that the customer would appear after she landed.

She circled a third time before setting down behind the island. Then she ran the Cessna out of the water, the wheels on the bottom of the pontoons grabbing as she touched sand and gravel, taking her up past the high-tide mark.

Still no sign of life. She might have been alone on the island. She got out and walked around the plane, looking up the hill through the trees and seeing nothing except a bald eagle perched on an equally bald tree.

Luke had to be crazy, sending her down here! If she had been thinking straight she would have suggested waiting until morning. After all, there was only another hour until dark, and what was the point of spending a whole night down here for the sake of an hour of daylight? She could have flown down at first light tomorrow. No, even if she had thought of that, she would have said nothing. She had been far too desperate to get down here, to find Matthew.

There would be an explanation, some kind of mix-up. She was on the wrong island, or it was the wrong day.

She would go up and explore, and if there was no one around, she would come back for her sleeping-bag. Then she would climb into one of those lovely outdoor hot pools and soak herself until the tension was gone. One thing she was not going to do. She was not going to let the tears come. He was gone, but damn it, Matthew Kealy was not untraceable! She would find him.

She knew that she was never going to forget him, that she wanted whatever she could have of him. Every minute, every hour, even if it ended with his going and her crying.

Shane might have an address for Matthew, and she could telephone Shane at the school from Queen Charlotte City. If there was no address, she could always turn up as an uninvited third when Matthew came to spend the promised day with Shane in November. But November was a month away, and an address would only be a mail-forwarding service that might take weeks to catch him. She could not possibly wait that long.

She could ask Luke to let her use the Cessna on her days off. Luke could spare the plane quite easily this time of year. She was almost positive that he would say yes if she told him why.

'Luke, can I take the Cessna to search for the man I love? I sent him away, and now he's gone, and I need him!'

Her words echoed around her, but she did not really care who heard or who knew that she was about to start chasing after the man in *Charmaine*.

Matthew would be in Victoria some time in November. Shane had told her that. So he would be heading south. First to Vancouver Island, then down the inside passage between the island and the mainland. That ruled out miles and miles of futile searching. She would find him. Port Hardy. Alert Bay. Campbell River. She would search all those places from the air, and the passages between.

She was a bit breathless when she reached the top of the hill. She had been climbing faster and faster, as if getting to the top would get her to Matthew sooner. She felt elated and optimistic. For the first time in weeks she had the feeling that she could do something to get control of her life again. She would find the man she loved, and she was not going to let herself think too much about the possibility that he would not welcome her when she finally caught up with him.

She was glad that there was no one on the island. She explored the cabin and found it quite habitable, then went back down the hill to secure the Cessna for the night and bring back her sleeping-bag.

Before dark fell, she made sure there was wood for the fireplace in the cabin, kerosene in the lantern. Then she took the towel from her pack and walked up the hill, away from the cabin, to the very peak of the island. She could see the steam rising in the twilight. There were any number of places to have a hot bath on this island, old claw-footed bathtubs placed here and there on the hillside to catch the hot water that flowed down all over the island. Despite the fact that all the baths were open to the outside air, some were located quite well for privacy, taking advantage of the natural terrain of the island to shield bathers from view.

If she was alone here tonight, she was going to choose the big pool at the top of the island, where the artesian well flowed up from beneath to form a large, natural bath in a location that looked out on the world.

She came out in the clearing where the round pool sent clouds of steam into the cool fall air. She hung her towel on a branch and added her jeans, her shirt, and finally her bra and panties. She felt a moment's flustered nervousness then, standing naked at the side of the pool. What if she was wrong, if someone were watching? No, she had searched the island. There were no dinghies, no boats anchored offshore.

What if someone came while she was bathing?

She trembled as a cool breeze flowed over her breasts, then she moved slowly into the water. It was crazy to feel so nervous. She could not find a safer place in the wilderness to spend a night alone. The island was too small to support deer or bear; and no one would have reason to land ashore here in the night.

The water was up to her calves, the warmth rising to conquer the coldness of the October night. Under her feet, the bottom of the pool was sandy and she found herself wondering who had brought the sand up here to line the bottom of the pool for the comfort of people like her.

She waded in farther, until the water moved around her waist; then she sank down and floated, her body half supported against the bank behind her, her eyes partly closed and watching the water from this incredible vantage point. Who had a bathtub like this at home? On top of a hill, looking out over the southernmost part of the islands, the water and the hills stretching away in a beautiful, wild panorama for the bather to watch.

She let her hands spread out over the water, arms floating and warmth caressing her everywhere. The wind was rising a little as the warmth of the sun left the world. The sounds of nature were all around, wind and birds somewhere hidden in the trees. Once, the wind made a noise like an outboard engine, and she felt a momentary nervous urge to scurry out of the warm water and into her clothes.

No one was here. She was alone, and not about to give up the wonderful luxury because she was actually a nervous girl and not a brave pilot at all. She pictured herself telling the men at QC Air that she had been afraid to have a bath alone on the island at night, and that settled the silliness. She stayed in the water.

When she closed her eyes she could hear a symphony of sounds that daylight had masked. The birds rustling in the underbrush. The ocean a slow surf on rocks that seemed far away, rising and falling, sometimes coming loudly as a larger, longer swell washed up over the shore. The wind, gentle, making strange sounds on the land and the trees.

She should do this more often, sharing the night sounds with nature. Her mind felt clear and tranquil, the problems and fears reduced to ultimate simplicity. She had a strange, almost psychic conviction that both Matthew and Shane were very close to her right now.

When the twig cracked on the path her eyes flew open, and she knew who he was before he came over the crest of the hill. When he stopped, a dark shadow against the moonlit sky, her eyes could see that he was tall and lean. She could make out the bulky shape of the unzipped life-jacket that he wore.

'Matthew...'

He heard her. It was dark enough that she was not sure if he could see her, but he came closer, and she knew his walk and the gesture that was a silent greeting. He stopped on the far side of the pool, standing with his legs astride, looking into the shadows towards her.

'Where——' The wind surged up over the top of the hill, blanketing her words, making her raise her voice to reach him. 'Where did you come from? Where were you?'

'Ramsey Island.' His voice had the impersonal tones of a chance encounter at the grocery store. 'I'm tied to the mooring buoy on Ramsey Island. I didn't like the look of the anchorage here. If a wind blows up in the night, I could find myself taken out to sea.'

'It's all right for a couple of hours here,' she agreed, 'but not for the night.' They were talking like two strangers, not like a woman bathing naked, talking to the man she loved. 'How did you get here? I thought I heard an engine a little while ago.'

'Yes. I came across in the inflatable dinghy.'

He had not moved since he'd got to the edge of the water, and she new that the flush on her face was more than the water. She was scared, terrified. There were words boiling up inside her, but she was afraid to say any of them. She was achingly, wonderfully glad to see him, and she was terrified of saying the wrong thing.

If he was here, there could only be one reason. He was here for her. But on what terms? If he came close and touched her, she was not sure if she could stop the words, yet she was terrified that declarations of love might send him away, or bring a cold reserve to his eyes.

She asked nervously, 'Are you—Luke sent me down to ferry some cargo from here to Lyell Island. I don't see any cargo, or any customer.'

'I'm the customer.' He sounded almost angry, or could it be nervousness in his voice? 'I—I asked Luke to send you here. I wanted to see you when I got back from Vancouver, but I—you were stranded on the mainland, so I asked—I waited on Ramsey, figured I'd get over here pretty quick in the inflatable when I heard the plane landing. But I was ashore, on the beach, because I'd decided you wouldn't be getting here today. It would be tomorrow at least. Then I had trouble with the bloody engine.' He shrugged, spread his hands in a wordless explanation.

'Why here?' Why did they keep talking? The words did not matter. If he wanted to be close to her, to have her near, she was here. He could come into the water and they did not need words. The words might separate them. She was afraid that words would tell him how much she needed of him, and it would be more than he could give. 'Why didn't you—why didn't Luke tell me to fly to Ramsey Island?'

'I—you might not have come if you knew it was me. You would recognise the boat—*Charmaine*—and—angel, I—I didn't realise you would be here. I mean, in the pool. I—angel, I——' He moved, shedding the life-jacket that he had worn for the dinghy trip. His head came out of shadow, into the moonlight, and she saw him push a shaky hand through the brown, unruly hair that he had forgotten to get cut again when he was in Vancouver. 'Angel, I—you said you hated my calling you *angel*.'

She shook her head, her hair swirling around her in the warm water, then realised that he could not see. 'I like it when you call me angel.'

He shifted a step back, turning to look out over the dark water below. 'I—I'm sorry. This—you're at a disadvantage. I didn't intend to put you in this position. I didn't know you'd be here in the water. I'm—angel, I'm really not trying to put you in an awkward position. I did arrange this, you and I here alone, but—I'm not trying to force you, pressure you into anything.' He was receding, back another step, and soon he would be gone. 'I'll go down to the cabin so you can—you can get out and dry and . . .'

Her heart was pounding almost as loud as his voice. It was incredible, but he seemed as nervous as she was. What was he afraid of?

'Matthew?' Her voice was breathless, urgent. He stopped, waiting, the life-jacket a dark bulk hanging from one hand. 'Matthew, please don't—don't go away.'

Had he heard her? She was not sure if she could ask again. What would he think of her? He had been the one pursuing her. Perhaps that was how he wanted it, and he would not want a woman who reached out and asked . . .

'Just to the cabin, angel.' He was speaking so low that she almost could not hear. 'I—I can't see you, but I can hear the water, and I—I can't imagine why you would have worn anything to cover you if you thought you were alone here. I—damn it, angel!' The words burst out of him like an explosion. 'If I don't get out of here, away, I'll—I didn't bring you here to force you into an affair!'

'Then why?' No, she was not going to ask, to force words he did not want to say, or to make him feel pressured. Had she not vowed to accept whatever he wanted to give, not to ask for more? 'Mountain Man, I wish you would just come here.'

She should not have said it. He was so still, so silent, and she felt horribly exposed, even though he surely could not see her very well. Her own hand in front of her was just a lighter shadow against the dark water.

He was going to go away, to leave, and she would have to get out and dress and go to him. Then it would be in his eyes, the knowledge of what was in her heart. She hugged herself under the water, aching for his silence to end. How long was it? A second? Two? For ever?

He was the man whose artist's eyes had seen into her deepest needs. What were words when he would see the truth in her eyes anyway? She had spent one night in his arms, and he had painted her as a woman she barely knew existed. He had seen her feelings, those vulnerable hidden needs, more clearly than she had.

'Angel——' His voice was carefully controlled, almost hard. 'Honey, I don't really have a hell of a lot of self-control. I—are you sure you know what you're doing?'

'Matthew, you——' Amazingly, she found herself laughing. 'Darling, I'm floating in this pool at the end of the world, and you're right—I don't have a stitch on. And I've just invited you in, so there's not much doubt about what I'm doing.' The laughter turned breathless as she said, 'And I remember exactly how little self-control you have. Remember me? I'm the woman who woke up from a nap to find you making love to her.'

It was only shadows, silhouette. His shirt tossed aside. His hand at his belt. The sound of a zipper. Then the jeans, thrown after the shirt. If she was a lady, she would have stopped watching then, but she didn't. She couldn't.

He was coming into the water, and she could already feel his touch, although he stopped several feet away, floating, close enough that he hardly had to raise his voice above a whisper.

'You asked me why this island, why not Ramsey.'

She moved the water with her hand, sent out a gentle wave that would reach him. 'You told me. Because I would see *Charmaine*. I would have landed anyway,

Matthew. I—before I landed here, I went to Rose Harbour. To see if you were there.'

'I didn't tell you the whole reason.'

There were too many words, too much of that tension that might turn to something else, keeping them apart. She pushed with her foot against the sand, felt herself floating closer. She ached for his touch, but he was holding himself still, his hands not reaching out.

Close to him, his dark shadow blanking out the moon, she discovered that she was more afraid of this strained reserve than she was of reaching out and being pushed away. He was not going to push her away.

Her fingers brushed his arm under the water, and she felt the reaction as his muscles jerked to her touch. 'Matthew, are you ever going to kiss me?'

He chuckled then, growling, 'I'm going to do a hell of a lot more than that,' and she floated up against him, and his arms were around her, bringing her close, softly, against him.

His lips were wet and she let herself drown under his touch, floating, wet skin sliding against his firmness, the wet curls on his chest lying against her soft whiteness.

It was a long, deep, drugging kiss. With the moon and the stars watching, it seemed that they promised everything with their lips; then his arms turned her and she was floating on her back, cradled against him, her head tucked into his shoulder and her hair floating around them both, lips only an inch apart.

Timeless, passion suspended, they were the only people in the universe. In the light of the moon, she could see the planes of his face and she reached up to touch his forehead, to mould the shape of his cheekbones and his jaw under the short beard.

'I could shave it off,' he offered, his voice husky as his hand gently traced the sleek, wet curve of her hip.

'I never really had a beard until I lost my razor.' He touched it with his other hand, then his fingers settled over the warm curve of her breast, stilled, as if waiting for something.

She felt the swelling that responded to fill his hand, the pressure of his touch against her hard, erect nipple. Soon he would make love to her. She could feel the wonderful, aching need growing inside her, alongside a timeless conviction that she could wait for ever, could be content for eternity lying like this in his arms.

'Don't shave it off,' she said, letting her fingers find their way through the beard. 'Tell me the rest of the reason why you had Luke send me here.'

His lips touched hers with an erotic suction, then he trailed a kiss along her cheek, her throat. Her head fell back against his arm, almost floating. Her fingers found the damp curls of his chest. He was silent, not answering, and she said, 'You don't have to tell me. You don't have to tell me anything.'

She reached her arms behind his head, drawing herself up and into his kiss. The water lifted her and they were close in a dizzying, spinning kiss that left her trembling against him, a warm wetness that wanted, needed, more.

'Luke flew me back to Rose Harbour. I asked the kid in the office for you, but you weren't anywhere around. When we landed, I told Luke—I said I had to see you, that I wanted a chance to be alone with you, away from other people and——' His mouth possessed hers deeply for a moment, then his voice was low and erotic against her ear. 'Angel, I want you so much. I've needed you for so long, I can't talk or think straight. I couldn't think straight then, either, trying to explain to Luke, but he's a pretty understanding fellow.'

'I know.' She shifted and felt his hard thigh pressing against her. 'I like him.'

Matthew seemed to stiffen. He said coldly, 'I guess he's pretty attractive.'

He was jealous. It might have been nice to savour the feeling of him resenting another man, but she had suffered too much from that particular pain herself in the past. She touched him fleetingly, reassuringly. 'He's a good friend of mine. That's all. It's never been more than that. Luke's madly in love with his wife. He's never even thought about another woman.' It was dark and warm, and his arms were around her. She whispered, 'You're the only man I want.'

He was very still, touching her, holding her without moving, his voice a husky caress. 'Luke said this was a magic place. He said that if we couldn't work out our problems here, there was nowhere in the world that would do it. He said——'

'What did he say?' It was boiling inside her, happiness, spurting up as if Matthew were freeing her, as if he loved her and would be hers for ever.

His voice was only a low whisper. 'He said that if I made you mine here in this pool, and told you I loved you, here under the stars, that you would belong to me for ever.'

She kissed him, her lips soft and responsive against his, feeling the restrained desire in him. 'Matthew, you don't have to say—you don't have to tell me you love me.' She closed her eyes, tried to tell herself the words would not make a difference. 'You don't need to pay any price or make any promises. I——'

'Shh——' His voice was a soothing caress, but his hands and his lips roused her, touched and loved and drew forth the wild needs inside.

'No, Matthew, let me tell you.' She could feel the hardness of him, the demanding male need to possess her, and she wanted to give herself, to be his always. 'I—Matthew, I'll be yours as long as you want me.'

He took her then, his hands guiding her, holding her hips, while he kissed her deeply, his tongue claiming the dark void that was his, and his body thrusting, entering her and making her his woman.

CHAPTER ELEVEN

HE CARRIED her through the darkness to the cabin, wrapping her in a big, fluffy towel and lighting the fire to warm and dry her. She lay silent on the sleeping-bag that he had spread out near the fireplace, watching him lay the wood and light the fire.

Then he came to her, drying her with hands that were soft and gentle through the towel. She thought that she had never felt so precious, so totally loved, as she did right now, with his hands touching softly, drying, caring for her, yet asking nothing.

Soon she would free her arms from the towel, stir and reach up to touch him, to pull his head down, his lips to hers. Then she thought that he would want to make love to her again, and she wanted him already. She lay still under his touch, savouring the knowledge of what would happen.

He bent down, kissed her, then brought the corner of the towel to dry the dampness around her ears. 'Sit up,' he instructed her, his arms helping. 'You've got to get your hair dry. Have you got a brush?'

'Somewhere. In my pack. I think I left it on the table.'

He went across the floor, his bare feet making a soft noise on the floor, his tanned back gleaming warm in the lamplight. When he came back, he sat behind her, drying her hair with a smaller towel and carefully brushing the tangles out.

'I believe that this is a magic place,' he murmured, brushing the damp hair away from her neck to press a kiss to her warm flesh.

She let herself sag back against him, felt the security of his arms holding her. 'Luke and Laurie were stranded here once,' she remembered slowly. 'There was a lost aircraft, a search, and somehow—I never did know how—Laurie ended up flying with Luke, helping him in the search, and getting a story for the radio station.'

'She's a reporter?'

'Yes.' She curled herself against his shoulder, turning. Her hair was dry enough. She wanted him to kiss her now. 'She's been on the islands all her life. Luke's the newcomer. I don't think they knew each other before that flight. They spotted the missing plane, then they had to set down here for the night.'

'And now they're married?' He kissed her, but she could feel the tension in him again.

'Yes,' she said, sitting up, pushing the damp hair back from her face. 'Could you give me the brush? I'll brush it.'

'Angel—Nicole, I——'

'Don't say anything.' She swallowed. Why had she started to tell him about Laurie and Luke? It was a love story, one that ended in marriage, and she did not want him to think that she was putting that price on herself. She wanted his love, whatever he could give. She did not want to trap him.

'I have to.' He touched the nape of her neck again. He had not given her the brush, now he started stroking her hair with the bristles again. 'I—angel, I want you to know that you don't have to be frightened.'

'Frightened?' How did he know what was inside her? Could he see through the darkness? Feel the trembling fear that grew in her when his voice changed?

'You keep running away.' His voice was very serious, very low. The brush moved steadily, but he had drawn back away from her. Perhaps he needed the distance to get at her hair properly, but the brush was the only contact between them.

It was true. Whenever he came close, she fled, afraid of the feelings inside herself. She managed to say, 'I'm not running now.'

'I don't want you to feel you have to.' The brush slipped through her hair and did not return. Only his voice now, sombre and quiet. 'I've been—I think I've been very unreasonable, angel. Assuming that you wanted the same thing I did.'

'An affair?' She stared at the fire, glad that he could not see her face, that she could not see his. Perhaps her voice did not tremble. 'I do want an affair with you.'

His hands possessed her shoulders, turned her to give him access to her lips. 'I want that, too,' he groaned against her, 'but I want more. I want——' She was shivering and he said, 'Please don't run away, angel, but I've got to tell you that I love you.'

'Matthew——'

He said hurriedly, 'I promise you it's not—it's not a trap for you. I won't ask any more than you want to give. If——' His voice broke and he buried his face in the half-dry hair that covered her shoulders. 'If you want an affair, that's what we'll have. Or a friendship. Or—anything you want. Just let me stay close, angel. I need you in my life, on whatever terms you want.'

His fingers went to her lips, silencing her before words could come. 'Please, listen, darling. I thought—I've never felt about anyone the way you make me feel. At first—hell, for a long time I didn't know what had hit me. The only woman I've ever been in love with is Gail, and it wasn't like this. When it came to a choice between Gail and going to art school, it wasn't hard for me to decide. After that—— There've been women, but nothing more than friendships, affairs. I've been lonely, of course, but it seemed better that way. I get to play uncle to Anne sometimes, and sometimes there's a woman for a while. A couple of years ago I invited a girl to come on the boat. She stayed for three months, and I was ready to murder her by the time she left.'

She saw him smile before he said, 'She didn't even do anything as terrible as throwing away my favourite Dvořák tape, but then, I wasn't in love with her.' The smile was gone and his eyes must have been very deep if she could have seen them in the firelight. 'At first I thought you were a beautiful woman I wanted in spite of myself. Then I found myself liking you in spite of my memories—half-memories, of that damned article. After I made love to you, I thought it was an obsession, and it took me a long time to say the word "love" to myself.'

She spoke through the fingers on her lips, telling him, 'Matthew, I love you. I do love you.'

He did not seem to hear. 'When I showed you that painting—angel, I didn't mean to frighten you. I wouldn't ever hurt you. I—I guess I wanted to tell you I love you, but I was afraid to say the words, so I tried to show you. Afterwards, when you ran, I ended up running, too. I just wasn't ready to face up to the implications of my love for you.'

She said slowly, 'Matthew, you didn't even like me very much when you met me.'

'I didn't *want* to, my subconscious kept warning me, half remembering that newspaper, but if you had smiled at me, I would have smiled back, and I would never have sailed away from Queen Charlotte. I had to get away from you or I would never have got any painting done.'

She giggled. 'I might have thrown your Dvořák overboard long before I did, then. I—have you replaced it yet?'

'No. That's what brought me back. I went into the music store, and they had the tape. I guess it was kind of a symbol in my mind. I tried to tell myself there were a lot of things I could enjoy in my life without you. I could have my music, as loud as I wanted. My painting. Freedom...I could go anywhere I wanted, without having to explain to anyone.'

She said slowly, 'Matthew, it's all true. I can't handle that music, and I wouldn't want to hold you back, to trap you, but I can't promise I won't because——'

His lips covered her words, a brief hard kiss that insisted on silence. 'No matter where I go, how loud I play the music, what I paint—angel, if you're not in my life, none of it will be enough to fill my heart. I want to stay close to you, however—whatever way will work. If I can't, I think I'm going to be a lonely man for the rest of my life.'

She was crying and his lips took the salty tears. 'No...please, angel, don't cry. I'm not asking you to do anything that you don't——'

'Matthew Kealy!' She pulled away where she could see him, trembling, her words not very coherent, but she had to stop this crazy idea he had. 'Will you please stop this? Will you listen to me? I love you. I'm not running away, or saying no, or—I was coming looking for you. When I didn't find you at Rose Harbour, I was going to ask Luke to let me use the Cessna so I could find you. When I came down that mountain at Tasu and found you gone, it seemed as if the sun had gone down. I've been trying ever since to tell myself that I'm perfectly happy with you gone, but only a fool would believe that. I dream about you every night, and even when I'm flying I can't seem to get away from you.' She smiled tremulously, said, 'I guess it's because I don't want to get away.'

They were only inches apart, words echoing around them until the silence let the sounds of the wind in from outside. She could not stop her trembling. 'Matthew, I'm not running, but I am scared. I love you so much, it terrifies me sometimes.' She swallowed. 'I wish you would kiss me, make love to me again.' With his arms around her, she could not feel anything but love.

He took her in his arms, admitted, 'I'm frightened, too. It's pretty sobering to love you so much that you can hurt me just by walking away. But I'm more frightened of being without you.'

Later, when they were both exhausted from their loving, they slept, then woke again in the middle of the night, when the wind was still and the moon bright. They got up together in the moonlight and, holding hands, walked outside. On the path, he swung her up into his arms and walked with her to the pool, walking in and sinking down with her into the warm caress of the water.

He touched her face, feeling the beautiful contours that made up the angel he loved, and he asked very softly, 'Do you think you could consider marrying me?'

She nodded, then, 'Yes,' in case he had not seen. 'Please.'

When she had married Tyler she had been a child, but she had known the details of her future, the house she would live in, even the form of her day as the wife of a lawyer who had plans to become a successful young politician. If she married Matthew, there was only one thing she would know, the only thing that mattered. That there would be love, both his and hers.

'Angel, we'll do whatever you want. We can buy a house in Queen Charlotte if you like. Go sailing in the summers, or whenever it works out with your flying. Or we can live on one of the boats.' Two of them, and two big boats. Somehow it was obvious that they had too many boats.

She kissed him and touched him with love. 'Do we have to settle it all tonight? I don't know the answers. Where I want to live, or how we should arrange our lives. I just want to be with you, and if you're sure you want to be with me——'

'For ever, my darling angel. Where you are, the colours are brighter, the sunsets more beautiful.'

His lips found the warm curve of her breast, and in the last breathless moment before she lost control and let her body call out to his, she said softly on a breath of laughter, 'There's only one thing to be settled. The rest can settle itself later.'

He took her nipple in his mouth, felt her gasp as his tongue caressed the hard peak of her desire. 'What one thing?' he asked, attending to the passion he was rousing in her. 'Do you realise how impossible it is that I could want you again like this after I've been so completely satisfied?'

His hand touched the warm centre of her, and he felt how much she needed him, how she loved him. When she was moaning in his arms, he allowed himself one brief moment to tease her with a lover's confidence. He drew back from her, his touch gentling, teasing. 'First,' he said, his voice a husky passion in the darkness, 'first, we have to settle that one thing.' His hands brushed her nipples and she twisted under him, moaning his name. 'Tell me,' he whispered, knowing that he could not wait much longer to make her his again.

She touched his chest, drawing her nails gently across the hard muscles, feeling how she could make him tremble with need. 'We have to settle what we're going to do about Dvořák,' she whispered, her voice a seductive invitation that he was not going to resist.

He bent over her, found her warm hands holding him, drawing him closer, urging his possession of her womanhood. He held back one delicious, agonising instant. 'I've worked it out,' he told his angel. 'You're going to give me a good Walkman and a pair of headphones for a wedding present.'

He did not give her a chance to respond with words. He made her his in the warm waters of Hotspring Island, and he told her that he loved her, under the stars, so that she would belong to him for ever.

Coming Next Month

#1215 FRIEND OR FOE Jenny Arden
Kira's late husband had given Glenn Mason guardianship over her stepdaughter, Heather—a fact Kira deeply resents. But his responsibility certainly doesn't give Glenn any right to interfere in her life—and sparks fly when he tries!

#1216 LOVERS TOUCH Penny Jordan
The only way Eleanor de Tressail can keep her promise to her grandfather to keep the estate in the family is a marriage of convenience to wealthy Joss Wycliffe. Only, for Eleanor, it is a case of love.

#1217 NOT WITHOUT LOVE Roberta Leigh
Julia's assignment is a challenge—to guard an engineer-inventor who has received death threats. Since Rees Denton refuses to have a bodyguard, Julia has to operate undercover as his personal assistant. But how can she watch over him at night?

#1218 WILD JUSTICE Joanna Mansell
Cassandra has enough problems coping with her overly possessive father, so she is furious when Jared Sinclair lures her to his isolated Scottish home for reasons entirely different from those he's given her. Surely it can't be just for revenge?

#1219 CHERISH THE FLAME Sandra Marton
Everyone's happy about Paige's forthcoming marriage to Alan Fowler—except his older brother, Quinn, who returns on the eve of the wedding. He tells Paige her father has been embezzling money from the Fowlers for years—and shocks her with the price for his silence!

#1220 THE DEVIL'S SHADOW Sally Wentworth
Her glamorous sister, Verity, spoiled Charlotte's early romance with Craig Bishop. Now, six years later, with Charlotte's dreams about to come true, Verity seems ready to do it again!

#1221 THE GATHERING DARKNESS Patricia Wilson
Nurse Julia Redford agrees to accompany her young patient Justine to her guardian's home in the Camargue. Julia has managed to cope with arrogant, overbearing Luc Marchal on her home ground, but once in France, Justine seems fine—and it's Luc who gives Julia problems!

#1222 BRAZILIAN FIRE Karen van der Zee
Chantal finds the sudden switch of life-styles from small-town America to the glamorous sophistication of Rio more than bewildering. She is even more puzzled by the cool, arrogant Enrico Chamberlain, who seems to hold her in such contempt!

Available in November wherever paperback books are sold, or through Harlequin Reader Service:

In the U.S.
901 Fuhrmann Blvd.
P.O. Box 1397
Buffalo, N.Y. 14240-1397

In Canada
P.O. Box 603
Fort Erie, Ontario
L2A 5X3

INDULGE A LITTLE SWEEPSTAKES

OFFICIAL RULES

SWEEPSTAKES RULES AND REGULATIONS. NO PURCHASE NECESSARY.

1. NO PURCHASE NECESSARY. To enter complete the official entry form and return with the invoice in the envelope provided. Or you may enter by printing your name, complete address and your daytime phone number on a 3 x 5 piece of paper. Include with your entry the hand printed words "Indulge A Little Sweepstakes." Mail your entry to: Indulge A Little Sweepstakes, P.O. Box 1397, Buffalo, NY 14269-1397. No mechanically reproduced entries accepted. Not responsible for late, lost, misdirected mail, or printing errors.

2. Three winners, one per month (Sept. 30, 1989, October 31, 1989 and November 30, 1989), will be selected in random drawings. All entries received prior to the drawing date will be eligible for that month's prize. This sweepstakes is under the supervision of MARDEN-KANE, INC. an independent judging organization whose decisions are final and binding. Winners will be notified by telephone and may be required to execute an affidavit of eligibility and release which must be returned within 14 days, or an alternate winner will be selected.

3. Prizes: 1st Grand Prize (1) a trip for two to Disneyworld in Orlando, Florida. Trip includes round trip air transportation, hotel accommodations for seven days and six nights, plus up to $700 expense money (ARV $3,500). 2nd Grand Prize (1) a seven-night Chandris Caribbean Cruise for two includes transportation from nearest major airport, accommodations, meals plus up to $1,000 in expense money (ARV $4,300). 3rd Grand Prize (1) a ten-day Hawaiian holiday for two includes round trip air transportation for two, hotel accommodations, sightseeing, plus up to $1,200 in spending money (ARV $7,700). All trips subject to availability and must be taken as outlined on the entry form.

4. Sweepstakes open to residents of the U.S. and Canada 18 years or older except employees and the families of Torstar Corp., its affiliates, subsidiaries and Marden-Kane, Inc. and all other agencies and persons connected with conducting this sweepstakes. All Federal, State and local laws and regulations apply. Void wherever prohibited or restricted by law. Taxes, if any are the sole responsibility of the prize winners. Canadian winners will be required to answer a skill testing question. Winners consent to the use of their name, photograph and/or likeness for publicity purposes without additional compensation.

5. For a list of prize winners, send a stamped, self-addressed envelope to Indulge A Little Sweepstakes Winners, P.O. Box 701, Sayreville, NJ 08871.

DL-SWPS

INDULGE A LITTLE SWEEPSTAKES

OFFICIAL RULES

SWEEPSTAKES RULES AND REGULATIONS. NO PURCHASE NECESSARY.

1. NO PURCHASE NECESSARY. To enter complete the official entry form and return with the invoice in the envelope provided. Or you may enter by printing your name, complete address and your daytime phone number on a 3 x 5 piece of paper. Include with your entry the hand printed words "Indulge A Little Sweepstakes." Mail your entry to: Indulge A Little Sweepstakes, P.O. Box 1397, Buffalo, NY 14269-1397. No mechanically reproduced entries accepted. Not responsible for late, lost, misdirected mail, or printing errors.

2. Three winners, one per month (Sept. 30, 1989, October 31, 1989 and November 30, 1989), will be selected in random drawings. All entries received prior to the drawing date will be eligible for that month's prize. This sweepstakes is under the supervision of MARDEN-KANE, INC. an independent judging organization whose decisions are final and binding. Winners will be notified by telephone and may be required to execute an affidavit of eligibility and release which must be returned within 14 days, or an alternate winner will be selected.

3. Prizes: 1st Grand Prize (1) a trip for two to Disneyworld in Orlando, Florida. Trip includes round trip air transportation, hotel accommodations for seven days and six nights, plus up to $700 expense money (ARV $3,500). 2nd Grand Prize (1) a seven-night Chandris Caribbean Cruise for two includes transportation from nearest major airport, accommodations, meals plus up to $1,000 in expense money (ARV $4,300). 3rd Grand Prize (1) a ten-day Hawaiian holiday for two includes round trip air transportation for two, hotel accommodations, sightseeing, plus up to $1,200 in spending money (ARV $7,700). All trips subject to availability and must be taken as outlined on the entry form.

4. Sweepstakes open to residents of the U.S. and Canada 18 years or older except employees and the families of Torstar Corp., its affiliates, subsidiaries and Marden-Kane, Inc. and all other agencies and persons connected with conducting this sweepstakes. All Federal, State and local laws and regulations apply. Void wherever prohibited or restricted by law. Taxes, if any are the sole responsibility of the prize winners. Canadian winners will be required to answer a skill testing question. Winners consent to the use of their name, photograph and/or likeness for publicity purposes without additional compensation.

5. For a list of prize winners, send a stamped, self-addressed envelope to Indulge A Little Sweepstakes Winners, P.O. Box 701, Sayreville, NJ 08871.

© 1989 HARLEQUIN ENTERPRISES LTD.

DL-SWPS

INDULGE A LITTLE—WIN A LOT!

Summer of '89 Subscribers-Only Sweepstakes

OFFICIAL ENTRY FORM

This entry must be received by: Sept. 30, 1989
This month's winner will be notified by: October 7, 1989
Trip must be taken between: Nov. 7, 1989–Nov. 7, 1990

YES, I want to win the Walt Disney World® vacation for two! I understand the prize includes round-trip airfare, first-class hotel, and a daily allowance as revealed on the "Wallet" scratch-off card.

Name ______________________________

Address ______________________________

City ____________ State/Prov. ________ Zip/Postal Code ________

Daytime phone number ______________________________
Area code

Return entries with invoice in envelope provided. Each book in this shipment has two entry coupons—and the more coupons you enter, the better your chances of winning!

DINDL-1

INDULGE A LITTLE—WIN A LOT!

Summer of '89 Subscribers-Only Sweepstakes

OFFICIAL ENTRY FORM

This entry must be received by: Sept. 30, 1989
This month's winner will be notified by: October 7, 1989
Trip must be taken between: Nov. 7, 1989–Nov. 7, 1990

YES, I want to win the Walt Disney World® vacation for two! I understand the prize includes round-trip airfare, first-class hotel, and a daily allowance as revealed on the "Wallet" scratch-off card.

Name ______________________________

Address ______________________________

City ____________ State/Prov. ________ Zip/Postal Code ________

Daytime phone number ______________________________
Area code

Return entries with invoice in envelope provided. Each book in this shipment has two entry coupons—and the more coupons you enter, the better your chances of winning!

© 1989 HARLEQUIN ENTERPRISES LTD.

DINDL-1